Gravetide

Gravetide

Carolyn McKnight

ST. MARTIN'S PRESS   NEW YORK

Library of Congress Cataloging in Publication Data

McKnight, Carolyn.
  Gravetide.

  I. Title.
PZ4.M15883Gr   [PS3563.A31773]   813'.5'4   78-3979
ISBN 0-312-34454-6

For Rod, *my* Fidus Achates
and
For Christopher, my other treasure

Gravetide

1

Each clod of earth struck the top of the casket with a dull thud. It had rained constantly, it seemed, during the whole of March, so that now on this fourth day of April the soil was heavy with moisture. The rasp of shovel, the muffled thump of clods striking metal, and the cadence of the pastor's monotonous drone were morbidly syncopated. Dimly, Lea realized her own body rhythms had matched themselves to these mournful sounds, her sorrowing heart beating slowly and her breath coming in short, shallow rasps.

"Poor, poor Sir Harry," she said over and over to herself. "Poor, dear old Sir Harry." She saw again his eyes: so blue, so kind. They were like her father's eyes, she had always thought, not only in color but in the tenderness they held for her.

How like today, Lea recalled, was that day almost three years ago when they had buried her father. Now, once again, she stood alone and bereft by a graveside. Only this time she did not experience the numbing fear for her future she had known then. Sir Harry had seen to that. He married her a scant two months after her father's death, sweeping aside her protestations.

She could almost hear the ringing, forceful voice he had used the day after her father's funeral.

1

"Marriage to me, Lea, is the only solution to your problem. Your father's small income has ceased and, I venture, your savings have been exhausted by debts—the funeral, maintaining yourself these last weeks."

"But, Sir Harry," she had protested in a small voice, "you cannot mean this . . . you're too kind . . . I promise you I'll be perfectly all right. You and Father educated me well, at least in the classics. How could the daughter of such a scholar not be well enough educated to find a position somewhere? And, I shall obtain a good one. You shall see."

Almost violently he had interrupted her, seizing her hands in a rough clasp. "No, no, my dear little Lea. I simply couldn't allow that. You are in *no* way prepared to earn your own livelihood. Granted you're well educated, my dear, but you're far too young and too beautiful to cope alone in the world. As your father's oldest friend, as *your* oldest friend, Lea, I could not let that come to pass." His eyes had softened and, gently, he had raised her hands to his lips. Then, in a thin, strained voice she had never heard him use before, he had asked, "You find it so repulsive . . . so repulsive to wed me, a man a few years older than your own father? A man you've known all through your childhood as a kind of uncle?"

That was precisely what Lea had been thinking. She had found it almost impossible to restrain the shudders threatening to tear through her body as she listened to his proposal. She couldn't—couldn't!—marry a man she'd always loved in the way she loved Sir Harry. Why he'd been closer than a "kind of uncle." He'd been a second father. She hadn't had the heart to confide any of those thoughts, though, much less the urgent feelings of rejection that had raced through her because Sir Harry had seemed curiously on edge, curiously vulnerable. But, vulnerable or not, he had persisted in pushing her to decide on marriage to him. One of his most powerful arguments had been his dependence on her, especially in running his estate lands, a job that had become almost exclusively hers and the steward's.

"What would I do without you?" he had questioned over and over. It had only occurred to her months later that there were any number of alternatives to marriage which would have filled his stated needs and her obvious ones. His sister lived at Gravetide and, thus, it would not have been improper with her as chaperone for Sir Harry to have employed Lea as a live-in secretary or aide or whatever he might have liked to call the position. Perhaps he'd thought of that option and dismissed it on the grounds of emotional coldness. Why hadn't he taken her, a nineteen-year-old, yet to reach her majority, as a ward? It would have bestowed almost all the benefits of marriage he wished her to have. But he did not propose either of those alternatives, only marriage, keeping at her until the reality of her situation, forced to the surface by his words, had shattered her rejection of him. That very day, then, Lea had accepted Sir Harry's offer of marriage and with her acceptance locked away the youthful, romantic hopes, the store of dreams in her innocent heart.

And now her gentle, generous friend was gone. Gone! His casket was almost invisible under the wet earth being spaded into the grave. Lea ached with grief, stiffened against it, and forced herself to hold her head high. To stem the tears that threatened to wash her cheeks, she looked up to the sky.

There had been a sudden shower during the long carriage trip from the church back to the family burial plot, and Lea was sure it would rain hard this afternoon, but now she gave thanks that there was a bright interval of clear blue sky for Sir Harry's burial. How she and her father and Sir Harry loved this part of England! She had thrilled to London when Sir Harry took her there on their marriage trip. And the first anniversary celebrations of the Waterloo victory which entertained them in Bath the past summer were thrilling. But there was no place like Somerset. Their precious stretch of land near the Bristol Channel made them doubly happy upon each return.

Seventeen years, Lea mused, almost eighteen years, she had lived in Somerset—since shortly after her mother's death. Death. She trembled. She had known too much of the terrible finality that was death. She had been but a bewildered slip of a child when her grief-numbed father had brought her to the small cottage at the edge of Sir Harry's estate that was to be her home until her father, too, was lost to her through death. How dimly Lea recalled any of her four young years with her mother, but how vividly she recalled every year of her life in Somerset. And from the first moments of arrival, Sir Harry had been part of it all. He and her father had been the very center of her existence and she of theirs.

With a start Lea realized that the service was over and the few mourners, mostly old friends from the village and faithful servants, were milling about.

"Lady Asher, may I assist you back to the manor?" Thomson, Sir Harry's oldest and most loyal servant, stood at her elbow. He had served his master since they were both boys. He had been major domo, secretary, confidant, though termed merely "butler."

"Back to the manor. . . ." How comforting those words sounded to Lea. She loved Gravetide Manor, the ancient house she had known almost all her life and lived in as mistress for what she could consider now only a very short time. "Oh," she thought in anguish, "fifty-three is too young an age to die!" She realized she must have said this aloud, for Thomson's voice answered her gently.

"It *is* a young age for one so possessed of vigor, but we must not mourn him bitterly, dear lady. He was the happiest of men and would want, above all things, for you to remember him that way."

"Thank you, Thomson," Lea murmured. She recalled her circumstances and her duty, and gave him a warm smile before saying softly, "Please give your arm to Lady Winifred and see her and our guests into the great hall. I shall be there presently, but want a few moments here alone before I come up."

The servant took a liberty he rarely allowed himself and patted her shoulder gently before turning to assist a stringy, sour-faced woman who stood tensely by a great, dark tree near the grave.

As graciously as her impatience allowed, Lea accepted condolences and reminiscences, thanked the pastor, and fidgeted until she was quite alone. Then, tenderly, she withdrew a chain of early flowers from the folds in her skirt and, heedless of the damage she was about to do her black gauze, knelt by Sir Harry's grave.

She cast her homemade tribute onto the raw, oozing mound. *Sit tibi terra levis,* she whispered. It was the same blessing she had spoken over her father's grave—"light lie the earth upon thee." She rose slowly. A sudden gust of wind violently whipped her widow's weeds into tangles about her ankles, causing her to stumble. But she was steady of mind as she looked down upon the simple stone marker: "Harold James Holmsworth Asher, January 30, 1764—April 2, 1817."

"Goodbye," she murmured. "Goodbye, my oldest and dearest friend."

2

For all the solid dignity of his appearance, Clarence Kerr was not too stuffy. To a large extent, he knew, his profitable practice as solicitor resulted from the poise of his bearing and the natural cast of solemnity into which his features had seemed molded from youth. He inspired confidence and he was well aware of it. Yet the Ashers—especially Sir Harry, whom he had known at least thirty years—were never misled by the facade. They knew it shielded a warmly emotional personality.

At the sound of a door opening, the solicitor turned from the window and smiled at the young woman entering the room. She moved lithely, with an air of grace and freedom he admired, and greeted him with outstretched hands.

"Oh, Mr. Kerr, how welcome you are! I am so sad not to have seen you since the funeral. It's been a month, has it not? And how we've missed you." Her voice was vibrant with sincerity, moving his sentiments and making him suddenly glad that he had good, if incomplete, news for her.

"And, my dear Lea, what a pleasure it is to see you again. Will you forgive me for so shamefully absenting myself in this sad time? I did so only that I might attend exclusively to matters of the estate."

"You're forgiven, of course, especially as you've done exactly what Sir Harry would have wished. But, come, will you take tea before we settle down to matters of business?"

They chatted easily, exchanging information about her life at the manor during the last weeks and his activities in London. The tea was excellent, and Clarence Kerr felt himself unwind into the state of contentment and pleasure he always experienced at Gravetide Manor. Lea's conversation, at once intelligent and relaxing, reminded him yet again of the absurdity of those who thought Sir Harry a besotted old fool for marrying a chit young enough to be his daughter. He knew, if they did not, that Lea had loved Sir Harry as tenderly and deeply as she had loved her own father. What the gossipmongers also did not know, perhaps Lea herself did not know, was that Sir Harry would have attempted a move of heaven and earth to make her life happy and comfortable, whether or not she had married him. On one point the gossips were correct: Sir Harry *was* besotted with his bride.

Kerr believed he could date almost to the moment the change in Sir Harry's feelings from affection for the child to love for the woman. It was on Lea's sixteenth birthday. Sir Harry had arranged a party, and, since those close to Lea were pathetically small in number and mostly servants, not friends, the solicitor had felt compelled to make the journey from London to attend the celebration. All had been the same with Sir Harry, Lea and her father, Julian Ellington, as on numerous other occasions when Kerr had been with them—until after the cake cutting. Refreshments had been served in the magnificent formal garden at the rear of the manor

when a warm May shower blew in to send them skitter-
ing indoors. Kerr remembered he was talking with Sir
Harry as Lea, shepherding a straggling guest, came
through the doorway. Her white muslin gown clung
damply to her newly rounded, womanly figure, and the
color was high in her cheeks. At the sight of her Sir
Harry stopped in mid-sentence. He gazed at Lea as if
seeing her for the first time and, Kerr thought, behaved
in an odd, constrained way with her for at least the balance of time they had all been together that afternoon.
It was only three years later, after Sir Harry had confided their wedding plans, that Kerr recalled the inci-
dent and attached to it the significance he now did.

Lea's voice broke into the old man's musings. "This
is perhaps business, Mr. Kerr, and I do not mean to
interrupt your tea, but have you had time to look into
the matter in London about which I asked?"

He frowned. "Yes, my dear, I have, and there is
progress in that quarter. But, Lea, do you think it really
wise to continue under the circumstances?"

"You mean because Sir Harry is . . . is dead?" She
shook her head sadly but firmly. "Had he not become so
ill, we would have begun the project the past month. It
would be underway now. He was quite in favor of it, you
know, not just to indulge me, but because he thought it
a genuinely good and happy plan. Oh, Mr. Kerr, I cannot turn away from it now." Her heart pounding, she
added, "It is my happiest prospect—and what else
should I do with an empty life?"

Kerr felt a stab of guilt at the distress his dampen-
ing question had put into Lea's voice and face. "Yes, yes,
of course you must do what you feel is best," he reassured her, but none too convincingly. "Now, let us get to
the matter of the estate. Most of the affairs are cleared
and, as you know, Sir Harry has left you fixed well

enough. There is the manor, unencumbered, with the income from the farmlands. You would do nicely on this alone, but there is, in addition, the separate fortune mentioned in Sir Harry's will." He put a gentle hand on Lea's.

"My dear, there is something of a mystery here. Have no fear, we'll track it all down and settle the business. I've no doubt of it. But at present we can't seem to locate Sir Harry's considerable capital, or rather what has become of it. It's his damnable secrecy. . . ." He looked up sharply. "*Do* forgive me, Lea!"

She laughed softly. "Pray, ask no forgiveness for speaking the truth. Sir Harry would have been the first to agree with you. He was shamefully secretive about that fortune." She smiled wisely. "It was, I think, his greatest eccentricity. Besides, he held such suspicions about his relations. . . ." Her voice trailed off as if she wished she had not opened the subject of the eccentricities and suspicions of her late husband. It seemed disloyal.

"Well, it is causing us a devil of a time, I must say. This much we have learned—about five years ago, early in 1812, your husband divested himself of his major holdings of shares. It was an uncertain period. Sir Harry was deeply disturbed by the high taxation on businessmen and the trade restrictions which the war with Boney made necessary. And he thought the conflict that year with the Americans was sheer folly. Certainly, dear, you must recall his near apoplectic condition when the Prince of Wales became Regent the year before. Poor Harry was sure the Regent was going to sink the whole of the British Isles."

Kerr's eyes clouded with recollection. Lea reached over and patted his hand gently.

"Yes, well"—he cleared his throat—"I myself helped

10

Sir Harry with part of the liquidation of his shares and business interests. I know he must have amassed an extremely large amount of cash, but never could I persuade him to confide in me how it was to be reinvested. 'Kerr,' he would say, 'you'll not approve, so I won't burden you with it.' How I wish—*how I wish*—that I had come by a way to force the information from him." He paused, a look of recognition in his eyes. "But, my dear, you were always in his confidence. Perhaps you know a great deal more about this than I."

"Well, of course I know about the existence of the fortune, but few particulars above what you know. When I conceived of the idea for the special project, which would take a deal of money, Sir Harry decided it would help pass the time until we could start it if he made a game with me of finding the hidden fortune. I teased him that he was treating me as a child at a Treasure Hunt, but it gave him such pleasure. He said he'd been thinking about this game for a long time and kept things back from me just so it might be played. The game was for me to try to decipher clues he prepared and thus to guess what the fortune was and where he had hidden it. If I had not discovered it by the time for our project to get underway, he said he would reveal all. So, you see, I hadn't much incentive beyond pleasing Sir Harry by playing at his game. Besides, I had so much to do as always, so much on my mind." She looked abstracted for a moment, then pulled herself up with a start and added, "It's been so long since I thought of all this—since before his illness—but I'm fairly certain the treasure, whatever form it may take, is here on the estate." Her voice broke. "Oh, I know you think it so foolish but we . . . he . . . no one thought his illness was *fatal*! Surely he would have told! No, no, that's not right. I should have remembered. I should have reminded him."

"There, there," Kerr interrupted as he saw tears form in Lea's eyes. "Only try to think, to recall something which will help. In time we will discover what he invested the capital in, for it is too great an amount to remain secret forever under our inquiries. Your efforts could considerably shorten the time and effort involved, however."

"But of course I'll try, especially as Sir Harry was as keen as I for our special project, so delighted to be using some of his fortune for it. Frankly, even now, I shouldn't be too interested in it, but for that."

"Yes ... er ... well, let's drop the subject of your project for the time being. There's a further circumstance of your inheritance of which I'm sure you have no knowledge, since I myself was completely surprised by it." He paused, and Lea fancied she saw pain in his eyes. "My dear, Sir Harry made a codicil to his will when the two of you were in London on your marriage trip. It was sealed in an envelope marked for opening only if he died before you were twenty-five years of age. In the codicil he named a certain Collin Mannings St. John, Sixth Earl of Dursten, as co-trustee with me of the estate until you reach the age of twenty-five. I can tell you I was astonished by this."

'A co-trustee! But why?" She understood now the pained look on his aging face and impulsively took his hand. "Oh, Mr. Kerr, don't for a moment think that Sir Harry distrusted you in any way. He had the utmost confidence in you and told me so any number of times. He must have had a very special reason for this appointment." She scowled. "It *is* extremely odd, though, for I think I've never even heard this Lord Dursten's name."

"Well, Dursten's a good enough man; a bit too hard and taken up with the amusements of society for my tastes, but an intelligent fellow. I've made his acquaintance since learning we were to share this responsibility. Peculiar that with all the ceremony that attends his title, as well as the responsibility to pass down his title and wealth to a son, he isn't married. That's neither here nor there, I suppose." He cleared his throat noisily, perhaps thinking of the irony of his comment because of his own bachelor status. "Well, it seems that in youth Dursten's father and Sir Harry were great friends, which may account for the appointment. The Earl was sent here as a young man to visit."

"Sent to Gravetide Manor? How could that be? I don't remember the Earl of Dursten."

"Nor does he remember you. You must have been just a slip of a girl at the time, perhaps eight or nine years of age, and the Earl must have been, hmm-m, I'd say near twenty. Told me he came two successive summers to stay with Sir Harry and that your husband had renewed the acquaintance when he was in London with you about two and a half years ago."

Lea searched her memory. A vague childhood image emerged of a tall, well-muscled, sun-soaked young man. She had admired his horsemanship. The picture was blurred, but a sense of jealousy accompanied it. Ah, yes, she could remember the young visitor who took Sir Harry's companionship from her, but the jealousy had been a short-lived emotion, for those were the summers she and her father had travelled to Shropshire to visit cousins and she had been glad that someone would be staying with their friend to relieve his loneliness.

"Well," Kerr interrupted her thoughts, "Lord Dursten will undoubtedly pay a call on you soon, Lea, so you'd best be prepared for him. Don't worry. I can manage him in terms of the business very well; he'll be no bother to you."

13

"Yes, but please don't tell him about my special project. An ... an outsider might not understand at all. Indeed—" she paused and crooked her delicate brows, beneath which large hazel eyes sparkled mischievously "—I fear you're having difficulty enough understanding it and think it wildly unorthodox."

He harrumphed this aside and was about to return to the matter of the missing fortune, when the drawing room door swung wide.

"My dear, I didn't know you were in here. . . . Clarence! What a surprise! I thought you weren't expected until tomorrow." The lady who uttered these words in a grating, high pitch, held out a blue-veined hand which Mr. Kerr obligingly crossed the room to kiss.

"Lady Winifred, you're looking extremely well." He secretly crossed his fingers to protect against the lie, a habit left over from childhood which none would have suspected in the stolid elderly man. In truth Lady Winifred never looked well. She had the opportunity to be a handsome woman, being slender and rather distinctive of countenance, but it was an opportunity never realized because of her temperament. She seemed to have emerged from the cradle with a deep grudge against humanity, which she had so honed and sharpened during the course of her life that now, at forty-six, she was a spinster with such a vinegary and whining disposition that no amount of physical beauty could have made her appear in the least attractive. For all this, Lea had never disliked Sir Harry's sister, but felt a pity for her which she took pains to conceal.

"Clarence, I do hope your early arrival doesn't signal bad news. There's no trouble with the estate, is there?"

Kerr cleared his throat. "Not at all, Lady Winifred. A trifling complication merely. Nothing to worry about."

14

"Complication?" Winifred's tone implied more a protest than a question.

"It's no surprise." Lea spoke quickly to relieve the solicitor's discomfort. "Sir Harry's game continues, Winifred. Though you and I were convinced he'd left the fortune, or at least the details of where to find it, in Mr. Kerr's capable hands, that is not the case. He is as much in the dark as we, and I'm afraid the treasure remains to be found."

"If there *is* a treasure," Winifred said.

"I'm quite certain there is," Lea said huskily. "Sir Harry would never have led me on. Never! That would have been a cruel hoax, something of which that dear, kind man was simply not capable." Even Winifred had the good grace to hold her tongue when she saw Lea's expression.

Lea shook free of the grief she felt beginning to press down on her. "You're staying at least the night, aren't you, Mr. Kerr?"

"Indeed I am, for I wouldn't miss one of Gravetide Manor's famous suppers for all the world . . . nor deny myself the pleasure of your company, ladies."

"If you are to have any supper whatsoever, much less a 'famous' one," Lea laughed, "I'd best see to its preparation." As she left the room she heard Winifred say, "Nigel will be *so* pleased to have company. He's been. . . ."

Lea leaned against the closed door. Winifred's perceptions of her nephew Nigel seemed forever off the mark. That young man, she thought, scarcely would categorize Mr. Kerr as any company at all, given his oft-expressed predilection for the glittering conversation of the London salons. Nigel was the third-born of Winifred and Harry's sister Isobel, a rather pathetic creature, colorless and quiet, who had borne a dozen children, only half of whom had lived past infancy. It was impossible to imagine what Isobel might have been like as a girl and how she had come to make a match with Patrick Carey-Browne. Her husband was as extroverted as she was introverted. Dubbed "The Ass" by Sir Harry and often called such within earshot, Patrick was forever in financial hot waters, the demands of his large family and his own personal extravagance far outstripping his income and ability.

Nigel had accompanied his parents and two of the other children to the manor for the funeral. Upon learning from Winifred there would be nothing for them in Sir Harry's will, the Carey-Brownes had departed in unseemly haste. But Nigel stayed on and showed no sign of leaving. Of course, Lea reminded herself, no one had encouraged him to do so.

Lady Winifred was immensely fond of Nigel and he was unique in that respect, for there was no one else of whom the spinster seemed fond at all. Lea had often pondered this relationship. It was odd. Nigel treated Lady Winifred very differently than others did. He was in no way deferential, made no attempts ever to improve her spirits, and was frequently brusque to the point of rudeness with her. He was in fact the only person who could not be manipulated by her moods or her words and who insisted on treating her with a sort of rough camaraderie . . . and worse. Lea shuddered at the recollection of the two separate occasions when, accidentally, she had overheard Nigel taunting his Aunt about a "nasty little secret." Winifred's tearful voice pleading that he stop had so upset and angered Lea that she had almost burst in upon them to put an end to Nigel's tormenting words. But she had restrained herself. For that private torture was queer, too, and inspired Lea to believe that even Nigel's torturing of Lady Winifred somehow pleased the warped woman. But how could Nigel's bad behavior be the secret to Lady Winifred's enchantment with him?

Lea roused herself. She speculated far too much about this relationship and she needed now to rush off to see Thomson and Cook about the wines and supper menu.

3

"But, I say, Lea, you *must* be able to remember some of the clues Sir Harry gave you."

"Yes, yes, Nigel," Lea answered, "if you'll only give me a moment to think."

In the pause that followed, Clarence Kerr relished a forkful of the cherry trifle Lea herself had made for him. He wished this topic had not come up to take away from his pleasure in his favorite dessert: cake redolent with rum, cherries tart and firm, custard rich and thick—all topped with fresh, sweet whipped cream. The solicitor's considered opinion was that Lea's trifle could not be equalled by any of the excellent restaurants he frequented in London. He glanced at Nigel.

It was remarkable, he thought, what a close resemblance to one another the Ashers bore. They shared the same sandy-colored hair, pale complexions, and eyes of a watery blue. Their physiques, too, were similar—all three being built along trim lines. But the characters and personalities each brought to these similarities changed them into quite different-looking types. Nigel stood just under six feet and was well-conditioned but blanched to a pallor which proclaimed him a gentleman of the indoor pursuits despite his muscularity. After an athletic youth,

Sir Harry had turned a bit portly, though his hearty good nature never changed and this so animated his features that they had appeared almost handsome. Mr. Kerr looked at Winifred and couldn't repress a faint shudder. Why did she insist on dressing so? Tonight she had chosen a most unbecoming dress which ill-suited her thin, stringy figure. Its pale rose-beige color made her look rabbity.

Nigel's behavior was short almost to the point of bad manners throughout supper. That had been annoying enough, but the intensity, the avidity of his interest in the fortune more than annoyed the solicitor—it unsettled him. He wondered if Lea noticed, too, and, if she did, what she made of it.

"Come, come," Nigel pressed impatiently. "You're holding out on us, Lea."

"I'm doing no such thing. The only clue I remember distinctly gets us nowhere. I'm trying to think of one of the rhymed verses I never solved."

"Give the clue," Nigel insisted, "and let us decide. It may have got *you* nowhere, but it may give *me* the answer right off."

"Very well. One of Sir Harry's rhymes led to the clue which was a verse from the New Testament. Matthew, Chapter Six, Verse Two: 'For where your treasure is, there will be your heart also.' But you see that only indicates the treasure is here at Gravetide, since both of us loved the estate so."

"Not necessarily," Nigel said. "It might have quite another meaning—for example that the treasure is buried beneath something heart-shaped. A window, perhaps, or a monument of some type."

"Clever of you," Winifred commented, "though I know of nothing on the entire estate that's heart-shaped. Do you, Lea?"

"I can't think of anything."

"We must search. It's obvious I'll have to organize this affair if we're ever to make any progress," Nigel snapped. "I'll begin in the morning."

"Fine. I'm sure we do need your skills," Lea said. She was aware of his overweening enthusiasm for any activity he generated and knew from experience that she must try to curb him immediately. "Please don't involve any of the servants or the workers, though. Spring is a very busy season for us farmers; we've planting under way on the south forty. Why poor Mr. Burton is up to his ears supervising it all. Even now he's off on a tour to inspect and help the outlying tenant farmers."

"Good Lord," Nigel exclaimed. "You should mobilize every available pair of hands. What's spading a bit of earth or sowing a few seed when there's a fortune at stake?" He was clearly exasperated with her.

She was about to defend her position, but Winifred's chimed agreement drowned out her words.

"He's quite right, you know, Lea. You shouldn't concern yourself with the business of the estate. Why do you think Harry insured his steward's salary so that he might stay on to run things for you? No *lady* bothers for an instant with such low and common matters." She let out her breath, a sound more like a hiss than a sigh. "And, I must say, it is a delight to be free of the presence of that . . . that field hand, Isham Burton! Why Harry insisted—and then you continued—his abominable habit of having that laborer at table is more than I can understand."

As always Lea bit back a retort. She had suffered Winifred's reproaches on these subjects daily for years now and had schooled herself to accept them with patience and without rebuttal. Lady Winifred indulged herself in continual, petty criticism of all those around

21

her, the shell-like brittleness of this habitual fault-finding having only one weak spot—Nigel.

Kerr's voice sliced into the silence. "I think our young lady is most sensible and intelligent in the matter of the estate, Lady Winifred. Your steward, Mr. Burton, is an excellent man and would undoubtedly run things as best he could under any circumstances, but a property in which the owner takes no interest, provides no personal supervision, does not prosper as it should. Profits are always low in such an instance, and Lea is wise to keep a sharp eye to estate affairs." He paused and looked down the length of the table to where Lea sat at the opposite end. He smiled. "And just look at her! Who could accuse her of being *un*ladylike in any way?"

Lea waved away the compliment, but she could not wave away the admiring gleam in Kerr's eyes. Several dozen candles in ornate silver candelabra on the table and sideboards cast a rich haze over the room and its mistress, enhancing her already remarkable complexion. She wore a spring green gown in the fashionable Empire style which set off her shoulders and her graceful neck while its color made pronounced the usually dormant green in her hazel eyes. As he looked at her, Kerr felt a quickening, an oddly optimistic sensation spreading through him and fancied he knew something of the effect she had had on Sir Harry. Further, he realized why her husband had strictly forbidden Lea's wearing of mourning, going so far as to have the prohibition stated formally, if eccentrically, in his will. In this respect Lea had broken only one vow to her husband: she had donned widow's weeds for his funeral rather than a gown in their favorite color, yellow, as he had requested.

"A very pretty tableau, I'm sure," Nigel said sarcastically, looking from Kerr to Lea, who held one another's gaze. "But we've strayed dismally. We were discussing this little game between Sir Harry and you, Lea. Explain again how it worked."

"As I've already told you," she said a bit wearily, "Sir Harry enjoyed making up rhymed pieces which directed me to sources that were themselves the clues. The sources were always the classical and biblical material my father and Sir Harry studied and which they taught me to understand and appreciate." She sighed. "Does that suffice, Nigel?"

"Hardly," he drawled. "I gather these 'sources' are all obscure Greek tomes and heavy Latin volumes."

"Only if you consider the Bible, Caesar, Homer, Plutarch and the like obscure and heavy," she shot back. "Many of us do not."

He ignored her thrust. "The rhymes you spoke of, the ones my uncle composed, they must have been written out. He wouldn't have given them to you orally. You saved them?"

"Yes, he did write them out. And yes, I suppose they're about. I can't recall throwing any of them away. They're probably in the morning room. We spent many happy hours reading and talking there."

Nigel rose abruptly. "That's that then. We'll adjourn to the morning room. You ladies may have your tea there, and Kerr and I'll take our port with you."

Lea tried to swallow her outrage at Nigel's high-handedness. "We *do* have a guest," she said pointedly. "Out of courtesy to him, I believe we should leave this matter to another time. Certainly it would not entertain Mr. Kerr to spend the evening trying to unearth Sir Harry's rhymes."

It irritated Kerr even to appear to side with Nigel, but the young man's doggedness aroused his concern and, he was forced to admit to himself, his own curiosity as well. He felt it better for the matter to proceed under his scrutiny anyway, so he, too, rose.

"Most decidedly it would entertain me, my dear. If you'd lead the way, ladies."

Taking Nigel's arm, Winifred proceeded out of the dining room. Lea lingered to have a word with Thomson and found Kerr waiting for her just outside the doorway in the great, dark-panelled hall.

"Young Nigel's dreadfully keen on this business," he said in a lowered voice. "I wonder if it's wise to allow him to become quite so involved."

She chuckled. "Ah, you don't really know our Nigel, Mr. Kerr. You're worried he may attempt to extract all the clues so that he may steal our treasure. Never fear. While he may appear that callous to you, I assure you he is not. Callow, only, and he'd never be able to pluck up the courage to steal anything, though I daresay he'd *take* as much as I or anyone else would give him." Her easy smile vanished, replaced by a look of determination. "And give him more I shall! If and when we find this fortune, I want to provide for both Nigel and Winifred."

"But Sir Harry expressly—"

"It's not that I disrespect my husband's wishes, Mr. Kerr, it's simply that in the matter of the treatment of his relations, I could never bring myself to agree with him. They yearn for independent means, and I earnestly wish to see that at least Winifred and Nigel get as much toward that end as the fortune will make possible."

They had reached the morning room door, so Kerr was forced to still the words on his lips.

Nigel was ransacking a fall-front secretaire when they entered. It was a rather new piece, Empire, bought as a present for Lea by Sir Larry, and she prized it.

Do be mindful of those ormolu mounts, Nigel," she

warned as she saw him rake the sides attempting to pull out a ledger.

"Oh, the devil take it! Lea, here, you come search the blasted thing. There are far too many small cubbyholes for me."

"It's an unlikely place for the clues. I use that secretaire almost daily for estate business and correspondence and I'm familiar with the contents. Let's look instead through the rent table." She moved toward a red leather-topped table. It had six sides, each with a drawer in it, and the drawers were labelled with ivory letters on either side of the pulls. These ivory letters covered the entire alphabet. They were in order—I through K was on one side of a handle of a drawer and L through M on the other. "Let's each take a drawer and whoever finishes first can search the others," she suggested.

"But what are we likely to find except old rent stubs?" Nigel asked.

"No rent stubs at all," Lea explained. "This table hasn't been used for its original purpose since I was a little girl. It's filled with all manner of scraps now. The rent records are kept in Mr. Burton's office. Sir Harry and I liked the table, that's why we had it moved into this room."

They fell to the search then, even Winifred displaying none of the disagreeableness that Lea had expected. On the contrary she seemed almost girlish as she checked through the contents of the drawer before her. But Nigel grumbled. "Nothing here. Nothing at all. Only the silliest things. Why do you keep these bits of rubbish, Lea?"

As he did not seem to expect a reply, she gave none. In fact, she couldn't bear even the thought of going through all the oddments Sir Harry had stuffed into these drawers and burning them or throwing them away. It seemed so final and so wrong to part with the little bits of translations, the quotations, the snippets of prose and poetry he had lovingly copied, then absent-mindedly stuck away for some unknown future use.

Nigel's continual grumbling and Winifred's regular clucks made a steady counterpoint against which Lea and Kerr worked quietly. Suddenly Winifred ended her part in the duet by bursting out, "Look! Look here! I think I've found something."

All three instantly gave her their attention.

"The paper's all scratches, but what I can make out is definitely in Harry's hand . . . and this little part of a verse is about treasure." She looked over the smudged parchment she held.

"For all that's holy, Aunt, don't just stand there. Read it!" Nigel demanded.

"Yes, yes," she agreed quickly. "There's writing every which-way on the page, but this seems to come first:
'Though this is not a Godly search
This search for finite treasure,
There is a clue, that waits for you
In a sacred, but apocryphal measure.'
Some lines have been heavily scored out below, but here is some more:
'Seek out the Church Book,
The most important some say,
Then with numbers six and fourteen do play' "

Nigel snatched the paper and spread it on the rent table. "Look at this with me, Lea, and see what sense you make of it." She leaned over the paper. Catercorner on the bottom of the page, written in emphatic letters was the couplet:
"'Tis not just for the game I do commend
You find Old Sirach and his maxim attend!"

"Dreadful lot of mess, if you ask me!" Nigel said. "What on earth does any of this mean, Lea?"

She shook her head. "Well, it's obviously a working sheet on which Sir Harry was drafting one of his clues, one he never got to finish." She felt a burgeoning lump in her throat as she thought of why he might not have got back to it—his fatal illness, the wracking grippe that made him gasp, achingly, for life's breath until he was forced to retire to the bed where he spent his last painful two days and nights.

"Let's get to work," Nigel said in an encouraging tone. He seated his aunt and pulled up chairs for Lea and himself.

Kerr spoke as Nigel settled himself. "Lea, my dear, I think it's really quite simple. He was directing you to the Apocrypha, was he not? 'Apocryphal measure' and all that."

"Yes," Nigel cut in, "but where precisely? There are dozens of books of the Apocrypha."

Lea read carefully over the paper, then smiled broadly. "Dear Sir Harry. How *chagrined* he would be to know we'd found this. You see, he hadn't yet come by a way to bury his clues. Yes, the Apocrypha is quite right, Mr. Kerr. And these words: 'Church Book' . . . '6 and 14' . . . 'Old Sirach.' In Latin Ecclesiasticus means 'Church Book.' It's also known as the Book of Sirach and considered one of the most important, if not *the* most important, of the Old Testament Apocrypha."

She rose and walked to the bookcases across from the mullioned windows, scanned the shelves until she came to one containing a number of old, beautifully bound copies of various editions of the Bible. She selected the 1611 edition which had belonged to her father, and opened it.

"Yes, yes. Here it is. Ecclesiasticus, 6:14. And it's

bracketed. Sir Harry must have marked the passage himself." There was stillness in the room as Lea paused to read the words to herself before saying them aloud:

" 'A Faithful friend is a strong defence;
and he that hath found such an one
hath found a treasure.' "

"Good Lord," Nigel snarled. "What utter tripe! That maxim tells us absolutely nothing." He balled up the blotched paper Sir Harry had written and threw it hard onto the floor. "What a pathetic old bag my uncle was! Not able to make a decent set of rhymes for his ridiculous clues and then giving clues that lead nowhere."

Lea felt a sudden, scalding fury. She could endure almost any of Nigel's scornful remarks or any carping from Winifred aimed at her, but she could not endure such slurs on her old friend. Nigel had gone too far.

"How dare you?" was all she was able to utter before storming from the room, not caring for once that her anger showed, that her exit might be considered childish, that she had a guest to whom she should attend.

4

The morning was unusually warm. The air, heavy with vapor, was almost visible and lay as a thick haze over the earth. Very early Lea had gone to the Yellow Garden. Her feelings were still ruffled from the night before and in this special place, this wonderful spot created just for her, she hoped to regain her lost composure. Besides, she worked every day, starting only at a slightly later hour, in her Yellow Garden.

Sir Harry had begun the garden when she was a child, designing it to please and amuse her. He had always maintained that Lea's favorite color, yellow, was a perfect choice, a perfect reflection of her soul and personality which possessed all the qualities associated with that color of sunshine. The idea for the garden and the preliminary plans for it had been a surprise on her tenth birthday. Sir Harry drew her into the preparations so it would be truly hers. Together, with only occasional suggestions from her father and a few pieces of advice from the head gardener, they had worked diligently to turn one of her favorite spots, an elevated and level area a few hundred yards from the manor, into an all-yellow garden. They had developed a pattern for the beds and borders in every hue of yellow—ranging from palest cream to deepest gold—and a pattern for the succession of blossoms that ran from earliest spring through late fall. There were even some golden aconites and pearly snowdrops to discover under the rare winter snows of Somerset. Everything that could be yellow was yellow. Many plants had been selected simply because their foliage and stems were some shade of the color, flaxen or palest chartreuse. Even walkways were paved with lemon-hued brick and paths were composed of ivory-colored pebbles strewn with chips in amber tones.

Through the years Lea and Sir Harry had perfected the garden so that now it was a showplace, but a demanding one, requiring as much attention as it gave pleasure. In good weather, until his illness, they had gardened together almost every day, a habit Lea continued alone, and they had managed for the most part without assistance. Only in the heaviest work had they called on help from the servants. And Sir Harry with Thomson's assistance always took responsibility for the draining and cleaning of the tawny marble-edged pool with gilt-colored stone basin, the focal point of the west end of the garden.

Lea had always found solace in her Yellow Garden. She had brought to it her young hopes, her adolescent dreams and hurts, her more mature worries and griefs. Sir Harry respected her privacy, taught the servants and family by his example to do so, too, and now no one disturbed her when she latched the gate behind her. On this leaden morning, she walked aimlessly about before picking up her shears. She pruned listlessly, her thoughts elsewhere.

She knew herself rather well and, thus, guessed that her anger with Nigel over his harsh sarcasm of the previous night was motivated partially by a deeply buried recognition that his words were tinged with reality.

There was truth to the charge that Sir Harry was a trifle foolish in matters exemplified by "the game." He renewed his youth in her, Lea knew, but that was on a deep level. In this area, his game meant he felt free with her to be playful, silly, even childishly so, without fear of scorn or contempt. Nigel's words rankled because they struck a nerve, making Lea feel that she had allowed an unsympathetic outsider to intrude into an area of Sir Harry's vulnerability. If one didn't love, one could criticize and make fun of any behavior on the part of others, and Nigel's judgments were made without love, without even affection for his uncle. While Lea could understand his behavior, she could not yet excuse it. Her grief was still too raw.

She sighed. There was, too, the weather. It was attacking her nerves. The heavy air oppressed her spirits as much as it pressed at her body. It was as if the atmosphere brooded—not in acceptable self-pity, but in menace. Perhaps, Lea thought, it was really simply the weather that made her so uncharacteristically irritable and unforgiving with Nigel. She would have to mind that and put forth more effort. Could it be the weather, too, that was responsible for the apprehension she felt? A kind of gloom mingled with mild fear that had settled on her in the night and was not dispelled, but encouraged, by the day?

"Absurd!" she chided herself aloud as she started toward the winding path of uneven stone steps that led down to the manor. Mr. Kerr would be having his breakfast soon, and she didn't want to neglect him this morning as she had so shamefully the night before. She really should not have left him in the lurch that way, she reproached herself.

Just as she took the last step which let into the formal garden at the rear of the house, a thunderous crash signalled a heavy storm to put an end to the tedious weather. A jagged streak of lightning froze in the sky and a few drops of rain spat hard at Lea before she reached the shelter of the covered back doorway. As she entered she heard the running footfalls and shouted instructions of servants dispersing throughout the house to close windows and doors.

She felt her spirits rise while listening to the sounds within and without the house. She had always been excited by sudden summer storms and, although it was only the beginning of May, the morning had been so hot and humid that it had inspired this unseasonable response in both the elements and her. She hurried to the morning room, closed the windows there, and paused at the final one to watch.

The beginnings of the storm were awesome—the sky crackling and bellowing with light and sound, the wind whipping tree branches into startling St. Vitus dances. Then, quite unexpectedly, came hail. Small hard balls of ice pounded into the ground, slammed against the walls and windows of the house, beat at the tall trees all around. And, as suddenly as the onslaught had begun, it was over. Only a few dozen spheres of compact snow dying under the swift-following downpour gave testimony to the unusual event.

Lea went out to the hallway. It was very dark in the house. As dark as night. The happy excitement she felt at the start of the storm vanished. Back came the vague uneasiness. A flash of lightning leapt at the windows behind her, bathing the walls in an eerie bluish-white. Then it was dark again. Why, she wondered, had she never before noticed how many concealing nooks there were along this hallway? How heavy and oppressive the mahagony panelling was? She had always thought the

house cheery until this moment and now it seemed
. . . ominous.

She groped through the inkiness toward a glimmer
of candles ahead in the entrance hall. Mr. Kerr was
there with Thomson. They were deep in conversation,
with Kerr doing most of the talking and Thomson reacting with what for him were rather emphatic gestures
and expressions. Lea felt, oddly, that she was intruding
and hung back in the shadows near the side of the staircase. It was several moments before Kerr, shaking his
head in negation of something Thomson had said,
caught sight of Lea out of the corner of his eye. His expression seemed strange, almost guilty, but that was
nonsense Lea told herself and swiftly dismissed the
thought.

Kerr moved to her side and spoke quickly. "Ah, my
dear, I was just getting the advice of your good Thomson. He confirms my doubts about the wisdom of travelling this afternoon. The cloudburst will be over soon, no
doubt, but the roads are apt to be knee-deep in mud, if
not washed out entirely in spots."

"Of course you musn't consider leaving. I won't
hear of it."

"Then I throw myself on the mercy of your excellent hospitality and thank the heavens for this excuse to
stay on with you."

"Glory, what a tempest," Lady Winifred trilled down
to them from the turn on the staircase. She took the remaining steps swiftly, speaking all the while. "Lea, do
you think the steward should have the roof seen to? It's
leaked before on the western side of the house. What a
wretched visitation on us! You know, of course, that the
grounds will be dismal for a week after this. Probably
most of the shrubbery will be in shreds and—"

"And the rain is grand for the soil, dear," Lea interrupted the fretful recital. "Come, you two must be ravenous by now, for I am. Most assuredly I am. Give us your arm, Mr. Kerr, one on either side, and let us scurry in to breakfast."

Thomson had ordered up a large number of additional candelabra for the dining hall. The room danced in candlelight and appeared almost festive. Nigel, they were informed, had elected to take a tray in his room, but even without him Winifred enjoyed herself under Mr. Kerr's attentions. They indulged in a leisurely meal, and the mood, while not merry, was pleasant enough.

The good spirits did not prevail long after breakfast, although the storm did. It had seemed a squall when it flared up, fated to be violent, but brief. As it continued, surprising them by its length while confining them to a few rooms in which candles had been lighted, they began to grow restless. They would separate, only to discover themselves gathered by accident once again in the morning room.

On one occasion when she found herself alone with Mr. Kerr, Lea seized the opportunity to persuade him to review the near-fully satchel of papers he had with him on her husband's business transactions. Persuading him was no small task for her. There was a tussel between them on such matters of which Winifred and Nigel were unaware. While Lea wanted him to expand on specifics so that she might understand first-hand, Kerr wanted to keep them closed. He might support her against Winifred on the matter of estate business, the management of manor lands and such, but he most emphatically did not support her when she wished to apply the same independence and vigor of mind in his area of knowledge and experience. Lea attributed it to the fact that Kerr's understanding of the unorthodoxy of her upbringing was sufficient only to permit him to accept her freedom in any area save his—where he reverted to the traditionalist he was at heart. She thought he wanted her to feel his authority, admire him and through ignorance remain subservient to him, the man of the law.

She had to cajole and flatter him into unearthing the documents and explaining them. It was difficult, but at last she succeeded in absorbing him in the task. They went deep into those papers relating to the possessions and investments Sir Harry had disposed of—and precisely when—in order to amass the "treasure." Was the hoarded-up capital itself the treasure? Or had Sir Harry used the money to purchase some mysterious treasure? The papers did not reveal, of course, the answers to these questions, nor did they address the reasons why he had taken these actions which had completely altered his investment strategy. Lea and Kerr could only speculate as before on the political situation and the economic restrictions of 1812—and Sir Harry's rather violent reactions to them—as possible causes for his actions. What neither of them wished to speculate about aloud was the streak of suspicion, the eccentricity of Harold James Holmsworth Asher and how those two qualities might have affected his actions.

Toward the end of the exchange, the solicitor again confided his worries about Nigel's zeal for finding the fortune. Lea had heard him out, but refused to dignify his suspicions with discussion. She could and did agree, however, with one point Mr. Kerr emphasized—Nigel was quite right in realizing that speed in locating the treasure was imperative. It was too unsettling to live with such an open mystery. Further discussion was stopped as Winifred wandered back into the morning room.

Conversation between the three lagged after a few moments, and it was almost a pleasure when Nigel joined them. He provided only the briefest diversion, however, and as the minutes ticked by and the winds and rain went on unabated, talk once again dwindled.

"Blast!" Nigel was on his feet and beginning to prowl the room. "This filthy weather has wrecked my day. I'd intended to start the search of the grounds for something heart-shaped. Remember? Spent the better part of the morning looking over the house with no result. There are some small heart-shaped insets in that oriel window in the great hall, but absolutely no kind of hiding spot anywhere near it nor on the ground outside. Had the earth spaded beneath. Nothing buried there."

He paced more furiously. Lea, Winifred and Kerr watched him intently. Winifred tried desperately to think of something helpful that would assist in the search. Mr. Kerr wished to turn the matter aside but could come up with no courteous way to do so. And Lea, though a bit ashamed of her thoughts, dwelt on Nigel's lack of apology, his seeming disregard of the insulting words he had spoken the previous night about his dead uncle. Nigel stopped near Lea.

"Well, have you made any sense of last night's business? That 'faithful friend' folderol?"

"No," she said in what she hoped was a quelling tone. "And I don't intend even to think of it today." She turned a pleasant smile on Kerr. "I seem to recall that you are a devotee of whist." She looked to Nigel and Winifred. "I suggest we play and have a concern for entertaining our guest."

Winifred demurred that she was not up on the game. Perhaps it was contrariness or a wish to ingratiate himself with Lea that prompted Nigel's advocacy of the game, but whatever the reason, he soon enough had them organized for cards, aunt and nephew paired against Lea and Mr. Kerr.

"Shall it be long or short whist?" Lea asked.

"Five or ten points to make a game is of little consequence to me," Nigel sniffed. "Let's get on with it."

"Long whist it shall be, then," Lea decided and dealt the cards. They had played only a few hands when Thomson entered.

"Beg pardon, ma'm, for disturbing your game, but there is a footman here with a message for you."

"Lord, man, can't you see to it yourself?" Nigel asked. "No need to pull Lady Asher out for such a trifle."

Thomson nodded in Nigel's direction, but looked pointedly at his mistress from beneath downcast brow.

"I shall see to it," Lea contravened, "and be only a moment. If you will excuse me, please." She bustled to the door before Nigel could comment.

"I am indeed sorry to interrupt, madam," Thomson hastened to explain as the morning room door closed behind them, "but the messenger comes from Lord Dursten—your new co-trustee, if I'm not mistaken—and I thought you would wish to attend personally to any communication from him."

"Quite right," Lea reassured the old servant. She tried to sound brisk to conceal her intense curiosity as she added, "Now let us see what this is all about."

At the side entry was Dursten's footman, drenched, and still dripping quantities of rainwater into a pool that had formed on the mat beneath his feet. He shuffled forward a pace at the sight of Lea to make his bow, producing an audible "squish" as he did so. The sound brought an involuntary bubble of laughter to Lea's lips which she hastened to stiffle out of consideration for the footman's feelings. Then she saw it was truly no laughing matter. The boy was shivering from exposure to the cool interior of the manor in his soaked condition.

"Here, now," Lea said to Thomson, "you must rush this poor young man into the kitchen for some hot tea and dry clothes."

"First I must give you the message, mum," the footman said.

"Yes, yes, of course, but be quick about it. You'll catch your death if you don't get warm and dry." She accepted a sealed piece of parchment which the footman had kept dry deep within his clothing and shooed him away toward the servants' quarters, calling as an afterthought, "Perhaps a tot of brandy for him, too, Thomson."

Lea slit the impressively sealed missive. The writing was bold and firm, but there was no knowing if it was his lordship's own hand or that of a secretary. The message, polite but brief, informed her that Lord Dursten was in the vicinity, presently staying at an inn after visiting acquaintances nearby. He would arrive at Gravetide late the following day. Were his visit to be inconvenient in any way, she was to return a message to that effect by the footman who bore his note.

"Well!" Lea exclaimed aloud. She looked from the paper in hand to the trail of raindrops left along the floor by Lord Dursten's servant and back to the note again, then shook her head. What kind of man, she asked herself, could send out a fellow human being, friend *or* footman, into weather like this while he himself remained comfortably ensconced in an inn?

5

It was only mid-morning but Lea felt tired, an unusual circumstance as normally she was overflowing with energy. She had risen at dawn to ride over the estate and see what damage had been done by the storm that she should call to the attention of Isham Burton, the steward, upon his return. Immediately after stabling her horse, she had gone to Burton's airless little office, noted the most important details of her survey and then forced herself to pore through the ledgers.

Contrary to the belief of Kerr, Winifred and Nigel, the Manor was not such a profitable proposition. Of the harvests between 1793 and 1816 fourteen had been terrible, a few decent, but two really good. It was only with the most careful penny-pinching management and by constantly introducing improvements that she and Burton were able to keep a going concern and eke out profits. Lea had no desire, however, to share her burdens with the others, particularly Winifred who would moan endlessly over any threat, perceived, much less, real, to her feelings of security. She churned quite enough complaints as it was, Lea thought, without the gratuitous provision of new raw materials.

Lea sighed heavily over the entries in the books for

"taxes." So high. Then, too, the cost of seed had risen shockingly while, despite the Corn Law of 1815 to stabilize the price of wheat, prices had been fluctuating wildly in that grain as well as others. It was difficult to decide when to sell and when to withhold from the market. They had made a few misguesses there that had hurt. And, overall, Lea was determined to keep their wage-laborers' earnings as high as possible and their tenants' rents as low as possible. It was not just sentiment over fairness that made her so resolute in this policy, but a well-formulated set of beliefs in incentives to production so they all—laborers, tenant farmers, and landlord—might do well, if not actually prosper.

She looked hard again at the cost side of the ledger columns. Would they be forced to reduce the dairy herd? The acreage under cultivation? She pushed optimism to the front of her mind. They would reduce nothing. They would continue to make a go of it. With Burton's help, as with the help of the steward before him, she would persist in winning the battles with cost and pestilence and taxes and weather.

Almost as long as Lea could remember, since she was barely able to ride a pony, she'd been involved in estate matters, going about with Sir Harry and the old steward as they attended to business. The adults thought it a game for her, but even in her earliest years she had never considered it a game. Her small serious face, intent on the men exchanging figures on yields, was universally considered lovable. Her slight body, bent in earnest study of the intricacies of a new plow or the treatment of a horse's strained fetlock, was found comical or touching depending on the observer. She never knew what a stir she caused as a little girl and how much talked about she was by the people on the farms, in the granaries, in the stables, by the merchants and tradesmen in the village. The affection she engendered as a child lingered into her young womanhood and grew to mingle with respect as she matured. And now these feelings the people harbored for her stood her in good stead as she carried on alone without Sir Harry's authority to back her up. It seemed to Lea that she had *always* known how difficult it was to deal with the vagaries of the elements, government policies, all the forces—she often thought the forces whimsical—affecting the very survival of the farmer, the dairyman, the landowner. Worrying, trying though it was, she found the work exhilarating in its challenges. Undoubtedly Sir Harry had perceived this, because not a year had gone by after her sixteenth birthday that he had not turned over more and more of the management of the estate to her. Her zest for these affairs fit in well with Sir Harry's lack of it.

"My dear," he had said so often with an almost boyish twinkle in his blue eyes, "you really have much more of a head for this sort of thing than I. And a much more patient temperament for dealing with all these piddling details."

True, she knew, except that the "piddling details" to which he referred weren't at all piddling, but the very essentials of managing the manor efficiently. Lea almost laughed aloud as she hugged to herself the sudden memory of the lovable, eternally youthful scamp Sir Harry had been. How he liked to play and how he detested coping with the business of earning a livelihood. Indeed, in those years before Lea had grown to the responsibility, he might not have earned a livelihood at all without the honesty and devotion of his former steward. Lea frowned. She'd been unhappy with Sir Harry's rather summary treatment of that faithful man.

In the spring of 1814, about five months before their wedding, Sir Harry had taken a brief trip, the purpose of which had never been discussed but seemed apparent when he returned suddenly with a stranger in tow. That stranger was Isham Burton. Only a few weeks passed before he pensioned off the old steward, replacing him with Burton. It was almost three years to the day since the younger man had become steward, Lea realized. She had no complaints about Burton. Far from it. She had only compliments and wondered what on earth she would do without him. After her marriage in September of that year Isham Burton had come . . . that year her father had died so tragically . . . Sir Harry had abdicated totally any interest in or responsibility for the estate. He was, he said, completely confident that she could handle everything magnificently with the young Burton to assist. And they *had* managed, Lea knew, though perhaps not "magnificently."

Weariness caused her shoulders to sag, but she straightened them resolutely, reminding herself that she always had Isham Burton to share her burdens on business matters and that he would soon be back at Gravetide. She closed the dreary ledgers and left the office to go to the house and inspect the preparation of the Oak Room for Lord Dursten.

At other houses the rooms were usually called by the colors that predominated in their decor, the Rose Room and the like, or by their position as if on a compass card, the Southeast Chamber. Sometimes, if a house had been honored by the stay of a distinguished person, a chamber might be known by that visitor's name, the Charles First Room or the Bishop Bedchamber. But at Gravetide it had long ago been established as custom to call the bedchambers by the names of the trees close by on the grounds of the estate. So, the Oak bedchamber it was for Lord Dursten. She had chosen the room for her new co-trustee because she believed it to be the finest one for guests visiting in the springtime. It had a splendid view of the meadow to the south of the house which was adrift with daffodils, cowslips and fritillarias. The blossoms, bruised and drooping from the battering of the storm of the previous afternoon, were beginning to perk up after a full morning of strong, healing sun.

Then, too, Lea had checked with Thomson and learned the Oak Room was the one used by his lordship when he had visited as a young man. She wondered if he would appreciate the familiar room or think it sentimental of her to have assigned it to him. This uncertainty was nothing, though, compared to the other questions about Lord Dursten buzzing in Lea's mind. Perhaps more than her active morning, it was these questions and her dread of the coming meeting with him, which were responsible for her fatigue.

She had been unable to sleep long after going to bed the previous night for she simply couldn't understand Dursten's appointment as co-trustee. What had prompted Sir Harry to do it? And why had he kept it secret from her? It was not typical of his behavior toward her. Why so uncharacteristic an act so late in life? It was as uncharacteristic as his not having left her or Kerr the specifics of the treasure—especially as he knew how eager she was and would be to get underway the project the fortune would make possible. She felt bewildered and impatient because not a single adequate explanation for any of this would come to mind.

When Suderanne, maid-of-all-work, came searching for her young mistress, she found her standing in the middle of the great Oak bedchamber, wringing her hands and staring down at the carpet. The servant was a big-boned woman, amply padded, but not stout. An old-fashioned mob cap, quite out of style, covered abundant salt-and-pepper curls. She was in her mid-forties, but she appeared a decade older and now the wrinkles in her face deepened and spread as her features puckered with concern for Lea. Suderanne had "done" for Lea and her father since they had first taken up residence in the tiny cottage near Gravetide. She cared for them as though they were her own family, and she had come to the manor with Lea upon her marriage to Sir Harry.

Suderanne did not like the atmosphere that had been developing of late, especially in these last two days since the solicitor had arrived with his unsettling *lack* of news. Even during the Master's illness there had not been the tension that she and the other servants felt now. There had been sadness then, especially in those last hours when it had become apparent Sir Harry would not recover, but not this indefinable sense of darkness, of something about to happen, hovering over the manor.

Fortunes. Fortunes just waiting to be dug out of the earth or pulled from a cranny in a wall. It was just this sort of situation, Suderanne thought, that brought out the blackness in the souls of people, blackness that might never surface but for such temptation. Her hands bunched into fists. She was angry all right. Silly old Sir Harry and his games! And she was worried. She had always prayed nightly for the welfare of her dear Lea, but recently her prayers had begun to take on a special urgency. For no real reason Suderanne could pinpoint, she felt afraid for Lea.

"Deary," she broke into Lea's abstractions, "I'm thinking you could use a nice bath and a little rest before you get ready to meet that Lord Dursten. Shall I fetch up the hot water?"

"What a good thought, Suderanne. A long soak will be just the thing, but I think I'd best try to walk off

44

some of my agitation before a bath. Be a lamb, now, and give me half an hour, will you?" She was into the corridor before Suderanne could respond.

Lea covered the twisty mile-long drive from the front entrance to the gates of the manor in brisk strides, all the while picking over the questions in her mind as rapidly as she picked over the ground beneath her feet.

Her major anxiety centered on the extent and degree of control Dursten would attempt to exercise over her affairs. If he were domineering, would Kerr have sufficient strength to check him? Would she herself?

It struck Lea with the force of a physical blow that perhaps she had never really known Sir Harry. Never viewed him through woman's eyes at all, but only through child's eyes.

She trembled and knew a curious sensation spreading through her limbs. Sir Harry was a keystone in her existence. Would everything crumble if her faith in him dissolved? She could not answer that question, but suddenly she could put a name to the curious sensation she was experiencing: fear. She feared loss of freedom at the hands of Lord Dursten, but more than that, she feared the uncertainty that had invaded her along with her first acknowledgement of real distrust of Sir Harry.

Lea turned back. She reached the point on the drive where it swept round boldly to reveal the manor, built a little more than two hundred years before of mauve-hued grey stone from a nearby quarry. The same stone "shingled" the roof which, like the walls, was very nearly obscured by ivy. Though familiar as the fingers on her hand, Lea had seldom failed when approaching the building to admire anew some aspect of its Elizabethan-style loveliness. But today she was blind to the splendor of the sun glinting off the mullioned windows; blind to the exquisite mottling on the pillars of the small Tuscan colonnade, drying unevenly after the wetting of yesterday's storm. She was so absorbed in her own emotions that she did not even perceive the clatter behind her on the sweeping drive until a carriage and outriders were well upon her.

She turned then and just in time to spring from the gravel onto the safety of the ornamental round of grass encircled by the driveway. The procession rushed past and onward the few remaining yards to halt at the main entrance. She recognized at once the servants' livery. She had seen it only sodden with rain and in the dim light of the side hallway the afternoon before, and it was much more glorious in the clear, bright day, to be sure, but the distinctiveness of its design and colors—azure with scarlet facings—demanded recognition under any circumstances.

A short, almost childish-looking man popped off a box he had ridden on the back of the carriage and hurried around to open the door. It was only when the passenger, the person who must be her trustee alighted that Lea became aware of her lack of preparedness for their meeting. Dressed still in one of her oldest and most serviceable riding habits of dull mustard-colored poplin, she knew she must look a drab wren, or worse. Before her stepped a peacock, impressively tall, wearing a coat of blue superfine and beautifully tailored pearl-grey pantaloons that disappeared into gleaming Hessian boots. There was nothing for it, Lea realized, but to face out the situation. She could hardly slink off, though she did consider doing just that for a fleeting moment. There was, however, no cover, no hiding place on the driveway.

Lea took a deep breath, slipped her damp palms down the sides of her worn skirt and marched toward the door. Her steps were not quick enough, however, to intercept the Earl. His flunky had raised the massive knocker as she reached his lordship's elbow, so that she found herself attempting an introduction even as Thomson swung wide the great carved door to Gravetide.

There was awkward confusion. The Earl, momentarily unable to comprehend that the windblown girl beside him was announcing herself as the mistress of the manor, turned to Thomson. It was that imperturbable soul who smoothed the situation.

"Your lordship, may I welcome you back to Gravetide? It has been many years since we've been favored with your presence," he bowed as he spoke in an unruffled, formal tone. "I am Thomson, Sir, and I see that you have met already my Lady Asher."

Lord Dursten stepped back apace to look down on Lea who had to throw her head back uncomfortably far to examine the face of the tall man. They studied one another. Her appraising glance matched his, but lacked its cold intensity. A frown creased her brow. All the questions she had been fretting over flew from her mind as she gazed into his eyes. The frown was not prompted by curiosity as to his character, but as to the color of his eyes. Were they grey? Deep grey like the sea after a winter storm? Or hazel like her own, but more changeable and without the lights?

The Earl's features gave no hint of what flitted through his mind. In fact, he was thinking that Lea was nothing less than a vision. She was dishevelled, but in a completely fresh and vital way. He wondered at Lea's powers to attract, reminded himself harshly of her highly suspicious position as the outrageously young widow of a well-off old man, and immediately hardened his heart against her as, even before meeting her, he had hardened his mind against her.

6

Lea squirmed. She was embarrassed and could scarcely conceal it. The meal was a disaster. Of all times for such a thing to happen with those narrowed, discerning eyes of Lord Dursten showing haughty disdain as each wretched course followed wretched course. Hundreds of meals had been prepared in the Gravetide kitchen since she had become mistress and not one, not even the most humble or rapidly assembled snack, had been poor.

It was the tension, of course, that was responsible for this awful food. Lea knew the servants had been in a tizzy over Lord Dursten's unexpectedly early arrival and the magnificence of his equipage and entourage. Poor Cook Runyon was certainly intimidated by what she termed his "consequence," citing as evidence the number of grooms and handlers travelling with him and for whom Lea had been hard-pressed to find adequate quarters. Undoubtedly, though, dear Mrs. Runyon had been completely undone by Lord Dursten's accompanying—and extremely arrogant—French chef who had poked about her domain, sniffing at the inadequacy of all he found there. Lea cursed herself for not anticipating the effects of all this on the Gravetide staff, the elderly Mrs. Runyon in particular. The cook was getting too old, Lea realized now, now that it was too late, to produce under pressure at just past mid-day the meal they had planned to serve in the evening. But it was not only Mrs. Runyon who was affected.

Something, Lea knew not what, had caused Thomson to fall down on the job of keeping things running smoothly. Astonishing. And almost as astonishing as Thomson's lapse was Suderanne's nervousness. Pressed into double-duty to help with the serving, the maid had dished up the soup early so that in addition to it being oversalted, it was tepid when brought to table. The fish had been undercooked but served with an over-held sauce Mousseline that had congealed into a glutinized yellow mass. The steak and kidneys placed only moments ago before them were encased in a crust so tough and soggy as to defy knife and fork. Now, on top of everything else, Nigel had torn it, absolutely torn it.

"Ghastly," he'd just snorted, pushing away his plate dramatically and letting his silverware clatter noisily onto the highly polished mahogany table.

"Perhaps you should let me resume supervision of the kitchen, Lea," Winifred said. "You're so dreadfully busy these days. And I did have the responsibility for many years, you know."

So, Lea thought, Winifred *would* whine out the implication that there never had been such a culinary failure under her watchful eye without even a hint that never had there been one under hers either. She clenched her teeth. Oh, what a delight it would be to throttle Winifred and Nigel. How dare they make the failed cuisine a matter of discussion! Had they but held their tongues this dinner might have been passed off with a brief word of apology, a small joke, and Lea could have taken quiet, private actions with the staff to calm and control them and prevent any further disasters during Lord Dursten's stay. A succession of good meals would have diminished, if not wiped out entirely, the memory of this horrid one. Now, unfortunately, she knew she was compelled to act immediately.

Nigel gazed at her balefully, as though accounting her responsible for a deliberate humiliation of him before Lord Dursten whom he openly and, Lea thought, cravenly admired. It outraged her that Nigel behaved as though this were his house and she his hostess. Winifred's smug satisfaction showed in the tight Cheshire smile on her thin lips and in the knotty cords threading her neck held stiff with gloating pride. Mr. Kerr could not force his eyes to meet hers. After gauging the emotions of the three she knew so well, Lea stood and looked down the length of the long table to the stranger. She wouldn't mince words, she decided.

"You must forgive me and staff. We are such rustics, you see." And, then, her voice dripping even more sarcasm than she had intended but which undoubtedly was stimulated as much by Lord Dursten's supercilious expression as by her own embarrassment, she added, "It is your 'magnificence,' I fear, that has set my household astir and caused this extraordinary fiasco of a meal. If you will excuse me, I shall see what is so dreadfully amiss in our kitchen that—"

Her last words were squelched by Dursten. He shoved back his chair and rose. "I can assure you I did not come here to enjoy myself." He cocked an eyebrow and surveyed Lea, who was at her loveliest in a fresh, clinging rose muslin gown. Where was the poke bonnet of transparent black material that was supposed to cover her springing, glossy curls? Where was the black shawl, a sign of mourning no decent widow in all of England would go without? But, then, she wasn't a *decent* widow, he reminded himself, and her failure to wear widow's weeds shouldn't surprise him in the least, only confirm his deepest suspicions of her. The matter of mourning clothes did ring some distant bell of memory, though.

Dursten's appraisal was so bold, so insulting that Lea's face flamed while her palm tingled with desire to slap him. His next drawled words seemed even more insulting to her. "No, I did not come here to enjoy myself in any way. I suggest we forget the rest of this meal, whatever it may be your cook has in store for us, and adjourn to discuss those matters of mutual concern which brought me here and which, if handled promptly, will allow me to take my leave with dispatch." He tossed down his napkin and moved away from the table.

Self-pity washed fleetingly through Lea. Everything had gone wrong with Dursten—their initial meeting, this meal. Why did it have to happen to her? But that emotion was swiftly transformed into fury as she watched Dursten's aloof progress toward the door. Why he was even more high-handed than Nigel who had played out a similar scene in this very dining room only two nights ago! Unexpectedly, for she had never before had such an urge, there welled up in Lea a wild longing to master Dursten. Not merely to overcome or subdue him, but to conquer and rule him. A delicious thought surged through her small frame. She imagined him reduced to groveling before her. But, quickly, her fierce anger at his pomposity drove out even that satisfying image.

"Lord Dursten," she rapped out harshly, "please return to the table. This is my home and I would not dream of letting guest or family leave my dining room so ill-served. I urge you to enjoy your wine while Thomson and Suderanne remove this latest offensive dish and while I attend to kitchen matters. *Do seat yourself*!" Her voice was shrill with command while her eyes raged at the provocative man who glared back at her. So hot was the contest in their locked stare that Lea fancied there might flame into actual sight the invisible line scorching the length of the room between her angry eyes and his glittering ones. There was utter silence as everyone, servants included, regarded the pair in frozen wonder at what either would do next. Lord Dursten ended their suspense.

"As you wish, madam." He inclined in a slight bow. The mockery with which he laced his words and the elaborate manner of resuming his place at table communicated all too well his perception of himself as the victor, not the vanquished, in the encounter. The Lady Lea, his sardonic smile announced, was something of an hysterical female and as such had to be placated in trifling matters.

"Please pour out more of the burgundy, Thomson—especially for Lord Dursten who has undoubtedly acquired an enormous thirst from having to converse with me." She spun on her heel and headed briskly out of the room.

Behind her she left a pall of silence. In contrast the kitchen on the floor below was seething with noise, but through all the hubbub, it was Mrs. Runyon's soft crying which came first to Lea's ears. The cook was demoralized. And one sweeping glance of the room gave Lea the cause beyond the bad food Mrs. Runyon had sent into the dining room. Dursten's chef. He stood in a corner, but he might just as well have taken the center of the room, so great was the dominance of his presence. Contempt radiated from the man. Like his master, Lea thought, transferring all her hot dislike for her arrogant trustee to his arrogant chef. Without the slightest qualm, indeed with satisfaction, she did to the servant what she would have liked to do to the master: she ordered him to get out and stay out of her sight . . . and out of the kitchen as well, she added as an afterthought. The chef banished, it was possible to begin to restore order.

Lea rallied Mrs. Runyon with sympathy and reminiscences of past successes. During this time she discovered that a young village girl who'd been hired as extra help during Dursten's stay had succeeded in preparing an attractive green salad. Lea had it dispatched to the dining room along with hot, crusty bread as the next course to be served during her absence while she was seeing to the rest of the meal. When the cook had braced up sufficiently, Lea extracted an inventory of the larder from which she selected some fine tournedos and early asparagus. She bolstered Mrs. Runyon to the tasks of lightly sautéing the meat and supervising the village girl in steaming the vegetable while her regular helper, Anna, prepared simple mushrooms to accompany the tournedos and a light butter sauce for the asparagus. The dessert, lemon sponge cake with drizzled icing, prepared well in advance of the ruinous furor of the last hours, was in excellent condition. While Lea herself was brewing coffee, Suderanne came to the kitchen after assisting in serving the salad. Her spirits were almost as low as Mrs. Runyon's had been.

"Oh, deary, deary," she moaned to Lea. "I'm that sorry about all this that I could fair kick myself across three farms! And poor old Thomson. Beside himself. Just beside himself that he should have let any of this happen. 'Course you know him, got it all locked up inside. But you can tell."

Lea put a comforting arm around her old friend and servant. "We've *all* let down miserably this day. I'm as much to blame as you or Thomson or any of the

54

others. At the first glimmer of this trouble in the kitchen I should have intervened. Instead, I shrugged it off and primped in my room while—"

Suderanne interrupted. "You're not to blame yourself. How was you to know everything was comin' down around our ears?" Her glum expression faded rapidly into one of glowering dislike. "I'm not trying to make excuses, mind, but if anyone's to blame around here, it's that bloomin' Blaecdene. Well and that Frenchie cook, too, I suppose."

"Blaecdene?"

"His lordship's valet." Suderanne spat the word "valet."

Lea was amazed at the disgust and anger on Suderanne's face, a face that almost perpetually showed the world a benign expression. It was so uncharacteristic that Lea was taken aback. "What of this valet?"

"Wicked-looking tyrant! All black beetle-browed and fierce-eyed. Got a club foot that makes a noise like a new broom as he walks with it draggin' along. I tell you that sweeping sound near sends shivers up and down your backbone. But, now, many's the times you'll remember that I counselled kindness about suchlike to you when you was coming up." She tilted her head in a thoughtful attitude and added, as if to prove her compassion, "No, you know very well I don't hold an infirmity against a person and Isham Burton's disfigurement has given me never so much as a moment's pause. But it's just that Blaecdene's foot along with everything else about his high and mighty ways puts you in a . . . well, in a kind of fear of him. Anyhow, it was him took Thomson off, Lord knows for what, otherwise Thomson would have been right down here putting a stop to what was going on in this kitchen. And that dark-eyed devil of a valet had me fetching gallons of hot water up to his lord and master and then complaining it wasn't enough and what there was was too cool so that I had to get Anna out of her work with Mrs. Runyon to help me and that set back the cooking."

"So his servants are as impossible as he is! I shouldn't be surprised." Lea's chin rose a fraction and set in a stubborn attitude, her eyes narrowed with determination. "All of us, Suderanne, will deal with the difficult Lord Dursten and his equally difficult servants as politely as we can. But, my dear, his wish, so rudely expressed in the dining room, shall become our one goal: to dispatch that man from beneath this roof with all possible speed."

It was a Lea filled with resolve who slipped back into the dining room. Nigel was telling a story, clearly trying to be witty, clearly trying to captivate the man who represented all he thought he would like to be.

As Thomson assisted her into her chair, Lea observed that despite the failures and the tensions of the last few hours, he presented the perfect picture of the unruffled butler. None would suspect the emotion she and Suderanne knew to lie beneath that surface. She felt ever so much sorrier for Thomson than she had earlier for herself. It was the first time in her memory that anything under his aegis had gone awry. She marvelled at his dignity and control. His reserve went deep, fathomless, Lea sometimes believed. Never did he intrude himself in any personal way, never did he reveal his own feelings in a situation. There was a kind of uncanny perfection about Thomson the servant. A shudder flicked through her. Strange. She couldn't imagine why it had come upon her. She wanted to toss off the queer sensation and accepted the first explanation that came to mind. It was a reaction of mere envy of Thomson's rigid control, a rigid control she most certainly did not own, but wished she did at this moment to help her deal with her trying co-trustee.

She dragged her attention back to the table, noting with some amusement that Nigel was finding it tough conversational going in the face of Lord Dursten's obvious indifference. She was eager to accomplish her new-found objective and waited impatiently for a ripple in the stream of Nigel's words. When it came at last, she wasted no time on niceties.

"Lord Dursten, I find myself suddenly ardent—as ardent as you express yourself to be—to deal promptly with our business. I see no reason for idle chit-chat when it was not a social purpose that brought you to Gravetide. Beyond meeting me, is there something special you wish to learn that you have not already had opportunity to learn from Mr. Kerr in London?"

He showed no sign of surprise at Lea cutting off Nigel mid-story nor at her forthright remarks directed to him. "It is very thoughtful of you to have a concern for the value of my time—and to respond to my desire for speedy conclusion of these matters." The sardonic amusement in his voice grated Lea's nerves. "I take it you have no qualms about discussing your affairs in public?"

"None whatsoever. And this is hardly public, Lord Dursten. Mr. Kerr obviously would be involved in any discussion between us. Lady Winifred and Nigel are acquainted with all the details of the estate and Thomson and Suderanne, who are serving, are close as family. With family or servants, I have no secrets." She waited for the impact of this statement, especially the reference to the servants, and was not disappointed. Lord Dursten's eyebrows rose. His servants, she knew, would never be privy to his personal or business affairs, not if he could help it. "So," she prompted, "you may proceed with any questions you wish."

"First, I should like to make one thing plain," came his immediate response. "Sir Harry's appointment of me as co-trustee fell out of the blue. I neither sought nor wanted such a responsibility. Indeed, when Mr. Kerr called on me to tell me of the codicil to the will, I was amazed. My own solicitors inform me that legally I can renounce the position into which Sir Harry thrust me without my knowledge or consent. And, in truth, it was my first instinct to do so. However, on reflection, I've decided against that course. The old man"—he punctuated the word "old" with a deepening of his already deep voice—"was a friend of my father and he was hospitable to me in my youth. I do not think that I could turn away from the responsibility with a good conscience—especially as Sir Harry obviously had a purpose in naming me. It is my moral obligation to fulfill his purpose, whatever it might be."

At this point Kerr, who had been muttering under his breath, spluttered into speech. "And what that purpose can be eludes me," he said hotly. "Sir Harry's affairs are in excellent order, excellent order. If you doubt, you may check the entire portfolio of papers in my offices." He paused for a gulp of air, his face dangerously red for a man his age.

"As of course you may check any papers here at Gravetide," Lea said hastily. If she could not remove the implication of distrust directed to Mr. Kerr, she could at least share it.

"Papers, certainly." Dursten dismissed the subject. His steely glance from Lea to Kerr communicated quite clearly his opinion of documents easily doctored to tell a pleasing story. "I'm much more interested in interviewing the steward here, inspecting the farmlands and dairyherds, that sort of thing." His eyes became slits. "But it is the anomaly of this hoarded-up capital of Sir Harry's—the 'misplaced fortune' I believe was the way Kerr described it to me—which is my imperative concern."

Like a schoolboy keen on hogging the glory of being first in class to shine, Nigel burst out, "Infernal lot of rubbish this Treasure Hunt Game, isn't it, Dursten? Makes me think old Harry wasn't quite right in the head those last two or three years. Maybe the will's not valid if he went off his bean, eh? That what you believe, my chap?"

There! It was out! Lea's stomach fluttered with nerves. All the silly details of the game with Sir Harry would be demanded by that judgmental, no-nonsense stranger at the end of the table. She saw Dursten stiffen.

"I am not your chap, nor you mine," he said to Nigel in a voice of awesome softness. "That is, by the way, a form of address that should be reserved exclusively for use by those in trade, 'chap' being a corruption of 'chapman,' a purchaser, a buyer, in case you were not aware." Quashing the attempt at familiarity of the young man he considered an upstart diverted Dursten's thought process for only a moment. Then he was honing in again, his senses alert, his face suspicious as he turned it toward Lea. "Treasure Hunt Game?"

"An amusing pastime for my husband, Lord Dursten. But one that has taken on the appearance of foolishness, even absurdity, since he died without leaving anyone the particulars of the nature or location of his treasure." Lea could hear the defensiveness in her voice and hated the sound, but much as she desired to erase it, she could not. "You must keep in mind that none of us, Sir Harry least of all, had even the slightest inkling of the seriousness of his last illness. A bad, but simple, bout of grippe. That was all. Even the doctor didn't suspect he might not recover . . . not until the last two days when Sir Harry began to sink so fast." Her voice caught in her throat. "During those final grim hours, my lord, I can assure you not one soul at Gravetide was thinking about anything except nursing him, praying for him, trying to keep him with us. Fortunes or treasure never entered my mind—nor anyone else's, I daresay."

Nigel moved restlessly in his chair and was about to speak when Winifred's bony hand fluttered over his arm in an attempt to pacify him. "It's quite true we didn't have a thought for anything but Harry there at the end," she said. "Though Nigel is quite right in feeling Harry's secrecy and his little game were folly."

"Sheer poppycock," Nigel exploded, adding the emotion he felt at Lord Dursten's set-down of him to his ridicule of Sir Harry.

"Yes, yes, my dear, the game most certainly was poppycock. I never dreamed my brother had been so remiss, so foolish in handling his affairs. Naturally I assumed, as any reasonable person would, that he'd left the details in his locked papers, safe with Mr. Kerr." Her watery blue eyes quavered over the solicitor, sitting across from her. "But you *tell* us you know nothing of the matter."

Clarence Kerr was wounded and for long seconds took no pains to hide it. He pushed back from the table as though it were an absolute necessity to have that additional arm's length of distance between him and his accuser. His elbows remained stiff, his fingertips dug into the napery, but his expression changed from hurt to outrage.

"You, Lady Winifred, you of all people, to launch such an attack on my integrity! To insinuate that I have withheld information and possibly for the worst purpose! I would never have believed it of you!"

"But Clarence, I did not mean—that is . . ."

Winifred's feeble protest drowned under Kerr's booming voice. "To set the record straight, Winifred, all of you, a solicitor can do just so much with a bull-headed client like Harry Asher. No matter that I was an old and trusted friend, no matter that I reproached him for foolhardiness, lectured—even shivved him with words—on his irresponsible attitude toward this fortune. He laughed. Laughed, mind you, and put me off, saying I'd not approve of what he'd done and he'd best keep me out of it. And that was the end of it. You may fault me, if you like, for not keeping at him, although I hardly think that persecuting him for the information would have been in the least effective, but you must *not* carelessly impugn my—"

"Dear, dear, Mr. Kerr," Lea stopped him. She was anguished that he had so overreacted to Winifred's quite characteristic tartness; it made him sound at the most guilty, at the least vulnerable in his handling of Sir Harry's affairs. "Please do not think you stand accused in any way by the Ashers. No one who has known you as long and as well as we could find any grounds for impugning your integrity. I'm sure Lady Winifred has merely mis-said herself, that's all." Lea turned beseeching eyes to that woman, imploring an apology, but Nigel spoke before his aunt had a chance.

"I for one believe you, Kerr. What you repeat as Sir Harry's words has the ring of truth. Sounds exactly like what the old geezer would have said. So, the fact remains that all we're left with are a few idiotic rhymes."

Lord Dursten pushed away his half-eaten dessert. It was a quiet gesture, but one he somehow made dramatic and that pulled the attention of all to him. At that moment, looking down the length of the gleaming table to the end where Dursten sat, Lea realized she had made a gaffe so serious and fraught with implication that it brought crimson to her cheeks. She had seated Dursten in the master's chair, the place that had been Sir Harry's. He should, of course, be at her right as the honored guest, because of his rank as an Earl, Mr. Kerr to her left, Sir Harry's place left vacant. She was so astonished at her blunder that she did not hear the words Dursten directed to her until he repeated himself more forcefully.

"I asked, Lady Lea, if I am to understand that the only thing known about this fortune is contained in a few clues from a Treasure Hunt Game?"

"Apparently," she mumbled.

"And you, Mr. Kerr, have you put out runners to investigate? If he cashed in his shares and other holdings as you told me, someone must know what became of the roll he pulled together."

"It was five years ago, Dursten. The trail is quite cold for the investigators whom I most definitely *have* engaged."

"Incredible," was Dursten's comment aloud, but his expression spoke many more words, Lea thought, words of scorn and suspicion, condemnation and disbelief.

"Incredible, yes," Nigel said. "But, then, so is the game. The clues are a lot of high-blown classical quotations located through gibberish rhymes of Sir Harry. Only Lea can decipher any of it. My uncle and her father thought themselves quite the scholars. Her father may have had some claim to being called one, since he had a chair at Cambridge once upon a time. With Sir Harry I think it was a lot of pretentiousness. Lea was trained by them in the classics—especially the ones they liked to go on endlessly about—all hideously boring, I can assure you. But she took to it from a little girl, always their willing and devoted pupil." He shifted his over-bright eyes to Lea. "How you could stand all that drill in Latin, Greek, all that drudge reading, painting, music, and Lord knows what else, I could never understand. But anything to please those two old codgers, eh?" He looked back toward Dursten. It was obvious to Lea that he was trying to recoup what he felt he'd lost with her co-trustee, even if it might be at her expense. "Good looks notwithstanding, our Lea is a regular bluestocking, if there ever was one."

"Bluestocking?" Lord Dursten's eyes bit hard into Lea. "*Or hetaera?*"

Lea went white with rage and shock. She felt as though she were trying to move through muddy water, thick with slime and seaweed, as she pushed herself up from her chair. She glared at Dursten until, at last, she found a choked voice with which to direct Thomson to pass the port and cigars.

"Lady Winifred," she said curtly, "it is past the time for us to withdraw."

7

Lea was speechless with fury. She roved her bedroom. She had stormed up the stairs, Winifred at her heels, and slammed the door so hard behind them that the window panes rattled and the ornaments on tables and shelves danced.

"Whatever is the matter, Lea? What was it he said that put you in this wretched swivet? I think I've never before seen you in such a passion. Honestly, my dear, you must try to control yourself, and you *must* contrive to be more gracious with Lord Dursten. He did have to suffer that dreadful food after the tedious journey here over muddy roads." As Lea glowered at her forbiddingly, she changed her tone and tack. "But, of course, what I really mean to remind you of is the fact that he is your trustee. It behooves you to get on with him, no matter the expense to your feelings. Well, isn't it in your interests to get on with him?" She paused, but when there was no response from Lea, who had resumed her wild pacing, Winifred reverted to her accusatory voice and expressed the real point she wished to make.

"There is Nigel to think of. You must try to be ingratiating for his sake. The Earl is so very rich, distinguished, holding such a position in society. Think of the entree he could give Nigel! You must not ruin his chances."

Lea paid not the slightest attention to Winifred. She was consumed by her own rage. "*Hetaera*," she burst out. She picked up a porcelain figurine to dash to bits in the cold fireplace, thought better of it as she'd never before thrown anything in anger, and returned the threatened ornament to the mantle. "*Hetaera*," she stormed again. "How dare he!"

"What *is* that word? Why do you repeat it so?"

Lea whirled on Winifred. "You do not *know* what an hetaera is? You do not know what your much-admired Lord Dursten has had the audacity, the insolence to suggest by his 'question'? Well, I will tell you. In ancient Greece, dear, dear Winifred," she spat out, "an hetaera was a woman who sold her favors."

"No! I can't believe it." Winifred's eyes popped.

Not giving a fig for once about the spinster's self-proclaimed "delicate sensibilities," Lea went on mercilessly. "Oh, yes, sold her favors indeed. An hetaera was skillful at pleasing men, tutored in all the arts, including the art of lovemaking. A girl was selected at a young age, taught from childhood for this . . . this profession. She was trained to converse intelligently, to entertain with grace, to seduce with skill—all to the end of being able to draw down large prices for her 'services.' I've read all about these hetaerae and it matters not to me that they were accounted to be among the most literate, educated, talented women of their time. Dursten's question was a hateful insult. Do you wonder that I could claw the eyes of that detestable man?"

" 'Claw' his eyes! More of that and I shall swoon. It is unthinkable for a lady to express a desire to do violence—even in reaction to a coarseness such as the one you attribute to Lord Dursten."

"What do you mean *attribute*? You heard him with your own ears."

"Well, I . . ." Winifred stuttered in confusion before turning cross. "I heard him use a word I do not know, that is all! I can scarcely credit the Earl of Dursten with being so crude, so unmannered as you make him out to be with your . . . er, definition."

Lea's mouth gaped in surprise and dismay. So Winifred, too, would sacrifice her to get on Lord Dursten's good side. She should have been prepared—she should have anticipated Winifred's treachery. Winifred, who was so concerned for her pet, Nigel.

The spinster continued, either unaware or uncaring of the effect she had on Lea. "Since yesterday afternoon when we learned the man was coming here, Nigel has talked to me of little else but his lordship's reputation. Dursten is in the first ranks of society, sought after by hostesses, a member of the best clubs, even, it is said, much admired as a friend by the Regent. All this despite a scandal somewhere in the family background of which Nigel has none of the particulars." She frowned before continuing in a querulous tone. "There is another point. Nigel is really quite as put out with you as I am for being so mum on this whole matter of a codicil naming the Earl your co-trustee. We should have been told instantly. Really, Lea, it was too, too bad of you. And then learning that even the servants seem to have known long before we! Nigel says—"

"Blast Nigel!" Lea erupted. Her bottom lip quivered and just in time she dammed the words that threatened to spill out. She was aghast at what she'd been about to say—a stream of reminder to Winifred that she and her beloved Nigel were at Gravetide on sufferance and would do well to keep their opinions to themselves and behave respectfully or else . . . Good Lord, what was

67

happening to her? She'd never conceived of Winifred's situation in such a light much less been tempted to say anything so unpleasant to the miserable woman. It was the fault of that dreadful stranger downstairs who was even now sipping Sir Harry's port. The hot and conflicting emotions he generated, Lea decided, were turning her into a shrew. She became conciliatory with Winifred.

"Forgive me for upsetting you, but you and Nigel have upset *me*. I cannot do battle with Lord Dursten while the two of you undermine me, if not actually go over to his side."

"There!" Winifred declared. "You betray the attitude that is causing all this trouble. 'Battle.' You set eyes on the Earl and instantly treat him as your enemy." As if she perceived much of what Lea might have been thinking and much more of the situation than one might have guessed, she added slyly, "If only you would attempt to win him over, it would forward the causes of us all, even Clarence. And perhaps you'd be rid of him ever sooner if you charmed him out of his suspicions."

Damned if she'd take pains to charm him, Lea thought, even if she could, and that was questionable. She doubted he was at all susceptible to her. He seemed to have taken a deep and intense dislike with that appraising look at their awkward meeting before Gravetide's front door. How hard his eyes had become as he took her in and, if possible, they'd become even harder, more condemnatory, when all assembled in the great hall for the mid-day meal. It was the second time he'd seen her, but the first as a well-dressed, well-groomed woman, rather than a dishevelled hoyden. What scorn had travelled from his rugged features with every glance at her delicate ones. And how horrible it had been and was still because never in her life had Lea known the least dislike for her person. It was bewildering and now, after his insolence, infuriating. She had to get that disturbing man out of her life.

An idea sparked by Winifred's words flitted through her mind and ignited on her face the first smile in more than an hour. Not "charm him out of his suspicions," but remove the suspicions altogether. Find the fortune, tidy up the loose ends of estate matters, and be done with Lord Dursten. If she were conscientious about written reports to him in future and if she were lucky, she might not have to pass so much as an hour face-to-face with him again until the time came, three years hence when she was twenty-five, for him to step down as co-trustee. Why even then? Certainly a "ceremony" wasn't required when she attained complete control of all of Sir Harry's estate. She crowed with happiness over her insights and began to race madly about the room, opening drawers and rumaging through their contents.

"Ah-ha!" she exclaimed after a few minutes of the fruitless search. Immediately she ran to the lovely Chinese marriage chest at the end of her bed and fell on her knees before it. She scrabbled at the brass fastening, then threw back the lid. Disregarding her usual neat habits, she started tossing the contents of the chest willy-nilly out onto the bed and floor.

"Lea, you're behaving so strangely. And you're making a terrible jumble of things. Whatever has happened to you?"

"The clues. I shall turn up every clue Sir Harry ever wrote. And I'll locate that treasure! The fortune itself can go to the devil as far as I'm concerned; the end result I cherish is ridding myself of that—" She let her words trail off in her absorption in the search. After a few more moments, she stifled an impulse to shriek with glee as she plucked out a piece of parchment.

A soft tapping at the door caught her rising hastily

from the floor, a look of triumph on her flushed face.

"Come in," she called gaily.

The door swung open, but the man who'd knocked did not enter. He stood uncertainly at the threshold, shifting from foot to foot, obviously shy and ill-at-ease. Isham Burton. A man as solid as the earth he loved so much and worked so diligently. Uncomplicated. Unsophisticated. The familiar sight of him was such a comfort to Lea that for the first time in their acquaintance she had an impulse to embrace him warmly.

"I hope you'll not think it too forward, Lady Lea, coming to your bedchamber. I guess it's only the second or third time I've ever been in this part of the house," Burton said, "but I, well, I thought you'd want to know I was back at Gravetide." His eyes struggled up from the carpet. "I have to be honest. A powerful sight more than that pushed me up them stairs." He forked a callused thumb back over his shoulder in the direction of the staircase. "I came back in time for the afternoon meal with you. But when I learned about that Lord Dursten arriving, I thought maybe I wouldn't be wanted at table." He looked meaningly at Lady Winifred before turning again toward Lea. "I went into the kitchen just after you'd gone and Mrs. Runyon shooed me out, so I took a plate up to the serving pantry. Heard everything that went on in the dining room. I know you were fierce mad from the way you left and then from hearin' your door slammed up here." He chuckled. "Gravetide's about the best built house I've ever been in, but even a mountain moves with a volcano, huh? I thought that whack you gave this door would slosh the port right out of the glasses of them three gentlemen down there."

He smiled broadly revealing a front tooth chipped in a childhood mishap which gave him an endearing boyish appearance that would last through old age and into his dotage. Lea took a hard look at his smiling face and knew that wordlessly he was offering himself up to act on her behalf in any way she asked. It moved her near to tears.

"Welcome home, oh, welcome home, Isham Burton. You've marched yourself back into the middle of quite a skirmish. But our forces shall win, never fear." She waved the parchment she held in her hand. "This paper and a few more like it, or rather what the papers will reveal, are our weapons. We shall be victorious." She laughed, staunching the lofty martial rhetoric she could have continued for minutes, so effervescent and exultant were her spirits.

"That one of the clues they was talking about at table? Like the one you found in the rent table in the morning room?"

"I don't see that's any of your business, young man," Winifred said in a high, astringent tone.

"It's his business as much as anyone's." Lea turned to the steward. "I just located this in the chest there at the end of the bed. Sir Harry gave it to me months back, but I'd forgotten. And, of course, as you mentioned, there is that clue we unearthed day before yesterday from the rent table, plus the one I remembered. That's a good start. If I put my mind to it, I'll find whatever others I kept or Sir Harry put by and forgot to give me."

"Never had much trust of the talk around the place that Sir Harry had a fortune hid away up here. You sure there's something to be found?"

"For once," Winifred commented with asperity, "it would seem Mr. Burton and I are of like minds."

Lea ignored her. "I'm absolutely sure there is something to find. As you've heard downstairs, there are all those shares and things he cashed in about five years ago. What became of them except that Sir Harry *did* convert them to currency or some other form and tucked them away where he thought safe? He never really trusted banks or brokers or such. And whatever form the treasure takes, I'm sure it's hidden here on the estate. Sir Harry wouldn't want it far out of his vigilant sight—and why else play the Treasure Hunt Game? Half the fun would be lost if the object were located in London or Bath or somewhere far away." She shook her head and smiled. "I can't imagine Sir Harry playing the game if not for the instantaneous pleasure he'd get from seeing me solve his puzzles and go immediately to get the fortune. Yes, it's nearby. I *feel* it."

"You *feel* it," Winifred repeated in a voice heavy with scorn.

Lea looked sharply to Burton for his reaction. His features were devoid of expression, his eyes slanted away from her. Rather than the compassion she usually knew at such a moment, Lea felt irked. With so much uncertainty and newness overwhelming her, she needed to have Burton meet her gaze levelly so she might read his eyes. Never a level gaze from Isham Burton! His head was perpetually cocked to the left, his ear no more than inches away from his shoulder. The source of this peculiar position should have been considered unfortunate, but not tragic as he made it through his shame. A huge port wine stain of a birthmark covered his lower left cheek and ear, poured down his throat and wrapped around his neck. Undoubtedly the constant list of head to shoulder was developed in a vain effort to fold that birthmark away from view and developed, too, at such an early age that Burton was no longer even aware of it. Lea had often wished to speak of it to him, but never dared, as it seemed too delicate a subject for him to handle. She wanted to urge him out of his embarrassment of that stain, to remove it as a blemish on his entire life. She pushed these thoughts away and took the immediate situation in hand.

First she must get Winifred out of the way and keep her from so much time for mischief-making with Nigel while freeing herself for her now more urgent tasks.

"You know, Winifred," she said as though deeply thoughtful, "I believe you were quite right in what you said in the dining room in the midst of our disaster. You must resume supervision of the kitchens during Lord Dursten's stay." Winifred demurred but, Lea noted, she preened as she did so. It took very little coaxing to bring her round to agreement that she would do a superior job. Actually it was because his sister inspired in Cook Runyon a red-faced hysteria half the time that Sir Harry had insisted Lea take over the kitchen responsibilities in the first place. She felt a moment's remorse at what she was doing to old Mrs. Runyon but eased her conscience with a firm reminder of the greater good to be achieved by making this assignment to Winifred.

"We'll want a supper tonight that's quite plentiful. See if you can muster something simple, but elegant, with Cook and Anna and that capable girl from the village who's helping out. But, Winifred, do remember—*ample*." Laughter gurgled in her throat. "Lord Dursten is going to work up an appetite this afternoon."

She turned to Burton. "And you, Mr. Steward," she said with a sparkle in her large hazel eyes, "prepare yourself for a strenuous tour and inspection. I've been over the ledgers this morning and they're in apple pie order. I rode about this morning, too. The farmlands, the dairy, the herds, are in a condition of which none could be ashamed. There's been some damage from the storm, but what of it? If Lord Dursten has the knowledge of these matters he would pretend to by asking to inspect us, then he'll know the damage to be of little consequence. And he'll be able to see for himself how well run the manor is. Off now and be ready for a message saying exactly when we'll meet you at the stable."

Winifred and Burton, leaving together, made such an unlikely "couple," especially since they heartily disliked one another, that Lea was smiling as she closed the door, this time softly, behind them. The parchment was still in her hand, and straightaway she went over to the Sheraton desk on the far side of the room to spread the paper on its beautiful inlaid top. Though she was in a hurry and couldn't spare time for studying clues at the moment, still she couldn't resist looking at what was there. There were four lines in Sir Harry's looping, childish scrawl:

'Meditate with the Roman,
Part named by your favorite hue,
Like and in the grove
We created, dear, just for you!'

The Yellow Garden! That was the grove they had created just for her. "But, of course!" she said aloud. It had not been simply for solace or out of habit that she had gone there the morning after Nigel's irritating performance following discovery of the clue in the morning room. It must have been a deeply buried, unrealized, memory of *this* clue that had added to her desire to be in that spot. She could think of nothing above ground in her garden that could harbor a treasure, so she concluded it must be buried. But where? They couldn't dig up such an enormous area—and ruin years and years of work in the process. And, besides, what would they be digging *for*? What *was* the treasure? Sir Harry must have given specific leads to its nature. She would have to ponder further all the clues and, especially, the meaning of the first two lines of this verse she'd just found. What could Sir Harry have meant by "meditate with the Roman"—and a Roman "part named" by her "favorite hue" at that? Why in the long list of "Romans" she could rattle off without the least difficulty, there wasn't a single one whose name, first or last, had anything to do with the color yellow!

8

"What do you *mean* he's off for a long walk?"

"Just that, my dear. We'd scarcely finished with one glass of port when he was inquiring about scenic spots near Gravetide to which he might walk. Said he needed the exercise and wasn't in a mood to ride. When Nigel told him about the view of the Bristol Channel from those rocky cliffs on your property about three miles over, Dursten said that would suit him fine as a destination. Abruptly, then, he left, saying he wouldn't return until well past tea time."

"Nigel went dangling after him, I suppose," Lea murmured, thinking aloud. She turned a vexed face back to Mr. Kerr. "Drat it all! I'd arranged with Mr. Burton to be available for a tour this afternoon. I can't tell you the urgency I feel to get that Dursten away from here. As far as I'm concerned, there's no conceivable way to move too swiftly to get our business together over and done."

"Calm yourself, Lea. I know you're upset because he was so offensive to you in the dining room. It shocked me. No matter what else I thought of him, I did believe him to be a man of rigorous politeness. After you left our company, he was almost as rude to me. Raked me over the coals for saying Sir Harry's affairs were in 'excellent order' after all that business of the Game had come out. So we're in the same boat on the score of Dursten's rudeness." He put a restraining hand on Lea who was moving agitatedly to and fro before him. "And there's no point in your running about helter-skelter, thinking a tour and the like will satisfy him instantly and get him off your hands. He's going to get his answers and that may take some time. So you'd best get it through your head that you're saddled with him. As I am. Oh, it's deuced awkward. Deuced awkward."

"It's a deal worse than awkward, I should say. Mr. Kerr, what are we to do? He's so hostile and rude, so suspicious. I am not spared, indeed I seem to be as much his target as you—though for the life of me I can't understand why he should be suspicious of me. His every glance at me since he arrived has been accusatory. Forgive me for saying it, Mr. Kerr, but I can understand an outsider's suspicion of others, even you. But me? It doesn't make any sense. Why, to think I'd hide my own fortune or pretend it was never found is ludicrous!"

"Not ludicrous, simple. Dursten doesn't know you, Lea. He sees a very beautiful young woman and knows nothing of the serious character and the sensible nature beneath that lovely exterior of yours. He may fear you want to do something with the fortune of which we trustees might not approve—gamble it away in the gaming hells, purchase geegaws and luxuries for yourself, any manner of irresponsible things. Perhaps he believes Sir Harry appointed him because I could not or would not control you . . . or worse, that we might be in league to dissipate the fortune."

"Bah to that, Mr. Kerr." She frowned. "Are you telling me I must have your approval and *his* approval for every use to which I put my money?"

"That is the very *raison d'etre* of trustees. I'd never

78

intended to do more than give a cursory scan to your accounts, Lea, I've that much trust in the way you run things. Now, with Dursten over our shoulders, I'm afraid I'll have to be much more thorough. Don't take it amiss."

"No, no." She waved away his warning because it was another matter that filled her mind. "How very peculiar of Sir Harry. He turned over almost all responsibility to me and *never* so much as inquired into what I was doing. Then, to institute all these checks and balances after his death—and for such a long time, until I'm twenty-five years old!" She shook her head in sad bafflement that ceased abruptly as she showed sudden alarm. "My project! My special project. *He* will have to know all about it."

She was talking with Kerr in the rather stiff formal salon where she'd found him alone after looking in several rooms for the men. Now she sank onto the closest of the three matched damask-covered sofas. For a long minute she didn't speak. "That unfeeling ogre will undoubtedly prevent the start of my project until I'm rid of him and my own mistress. Still, much as I loathe the idea of Lord Dursten learning about it, I suppose I must try to gain his approval—but not immediately, not until we've located the treasure. With that suspicion out of his mind, he may be more receptive to my plans for using some of those resources. First, though, I must try to win you over to my side, because you are not on my side in this matter, are you, Mr. Kerr?"

"What you plan is most unconventional. And I fear the consequences, Lea. Who knows how these little scraps you intend to pick up and bring into your own lovely home will turn out? I am of the firm belief that blood will tell, and the Almighty only knows what blood runs through the veins of the likes of them."

She sighed heavily. "There is no really rational,

satisfactory counter to your argument, I know. And you're right to bring the Almighty into it, for it is rather like a religious question that one must answer on the basis of a leap to faith. No one knows whether it is the blood or the raising—or a little of both, as I believe—that determines how one turns out in this life." She sought to lighten their talk and said mischievously, "There is undoubtedly, however, a vast amount of the blood of the peerage and the gentry running through the veins of the orphans in our country." She patted the cushion next to her. "But come, Mr. Kerr, let me explain how the idea for my project came about. Perhaps you can understand, if not sympathize and agree."

"Well," he blustered, "understand, perhaps." He took the place next to her as she'd indicated she wished him to do.

"The beginnings are in my marriage trip to London. Sir Harry and I were out riding in an open landau he'd rented and was driving himself. London had changed since he'd known the city well in his youth and after touring about Hyde Park and the surrounding areas, he lost his way. We found ourselves driving through a wretched slum. Sir Harry had pulled to a halt to get his bearings from a street map when I saw an infant swaddled in filthy rags, lying in a gutter not three yards away from us. I leaped out of the carriage and went to the poor little creature who was screaming lustily. We tried to stop people on the street to find out where the tiny chap might belong, but the few who would speak to us hooted with scorn or shuffled away after a sentence or two. If not infanticide, abandonment—we learned most hardly from our experience that either was a common course with the many, many unwanted children in those horrid impoverished areas. So we had the infant on our hands and not the least idea what to do with him."

"You should have left him where you found him. His fate was none of your concern."

"Mr. Kerr!" she exclaimed in disbelief. "We couldn't leave a helpless, defenseless little baby to die in a gutter." She stared at him. There was tenderness, she knew, beneath the sterness he affected and she decided to call him on this issue. "I would be willing to wager all I have that you could *not* have abandoned that infant had you found him. Truth to tell, Mr. Kerr, could you really have left anyone, child or adult, rich or poor, in such a dire position?"

He grumbled, shaking his head just enough to set his jowls atremble.

"Could you?" she prompted.

"I suppose not," he conceded grudgingly.

"Certainly not, no more than we," she said with satisfaction. "Now, where was I? Oh, yes, there we were with the babe in my arms, at last succeeding in finding our way back to our hotel. I can tell you we caused quite a stir when we arrived in the lobby with that grubby little fellow. But people were surprisingly kind and upon inquiry we learned we might take the child to a foundling hospital in the northern fields. It's called the Lambeth House of Asylum." She snapped her fingers. "How forgetful of me. Of course you know all that, as you've been there on my behalf."

"Well, not exactly. My only contact has been through written communication with staff."

Lea stifled words of disappointment in his handling of her request. She could have written; it was because he was located in London that she had involved him at all. She thought she'd made clear her expectation that he would expedite her cause through personal appeal. There was a hint of reproach in her voice when she spoke again. "Perhaps if you had gone to Lambeth

House you might better understand my feelings in this matter. The place is full of children of all ages, deserted or left bereft. Oh, it's quite clean, though sparsely furnished and lighted, and the children look well, all neatly turned out in white tuckers and purple clothing. But it's so spartan. And such an emphasis on industry—menial industry. The children are taught mostly the work of house and kitchen, though they are instructed in the rudiments of reading, writing and numbers. Then at age fifteen they're apprenticed out for seven years to families approved by the governors."

"It sounds a decent enough place for the unwanted brats of the poor. Why not have left the matter there, Lea?"

"You haven't heard or felt a scintilla of the emotion behind my words, have you, Mr. Kerr? The memory of that babe and of all the children I saw at Lambeth House stayed with me—unshakable recollections of the adequate care they received, but the lack of cheer and hope and love." She shuddered. "So practical, but so austere. I could never forget it. One day, perhaps a little more than six months before Sir Harry died, the idea came to me that I might have the large family for which I yearned and satisfy my conscience about those children by adopting a family out of Lambeth."

Kerr dared not ask why she and Sir Harry hadn't started a family of their own. And, although he thought he knew the answer to another question that came to mind—an answer based on the notion that the doting Sir Harry would deny Lea nothing she wanted—still he asked, "And Harry was *for* this scheme?"

"Indeed he was." She turned her face away so he might not see the stain spreading over her cheeks. She had told the truth. Sir Harry had been most enthusiastic about the idea, but it was the circumstance of their life together as man and wife that, she knew, had promoted his enthusiasm and caused now her color to rise. But she couldn't possibly go into that with Kerr—or anyone else. "Yes, yes, Sir Harry was for it," she said quickly to cover her questionable pause. "He helped me with the details. I had correspondence with Matron at Lambeth about the feasibility of my plan. She assured me it was entirely possible—they always have too many children and too few resources and are glad of the opportunity to place some of the little ones. We had only to meet two requirements: to show financial solvency and to submit to an inspection by at least one of the members of their Board of Governors. Obviously a landholder like Sir Harry met the former requirement easily, and it was nothing to get high marks from the governors who came to look over Gravetide." She chuckled. "Those two gentlemen were so obviously delighted to have an excuse to escape London and visit awhile in our lovely Somerset!"

"Winifred is adamantly opposed to your plan, you know. She's spoken to me about it."

"I think she may change her mind once the babes are actually here. I hope she will, but whether or not she does is of little consequence. She may keep out of their way, and I shall arrange to have them kept out of hers. Suderanne is thrilled about the idea. And we would hire extra help, a couple of young women from the village. We've applied for only three little ones to start, but even three are such a lot of additional work. And they cost money, money I can't spare from the household accounts or withdraw from the pool set aside for improvements to the land and dairy herds. So, I must find Sir Harry's treasure. And I must know if you will stand with me or against me in this venture, Mr. Kerr."

"While I cannot be brought round to your philosophy or to a belief that your undertaking is felicitous,

I will not bar use of your funds for such a purpose. It is, I suppose, what another might consider 'worthy.' Certainly it is no frivolity."

"Thank you, Mr. Kerr. I might wish you to be in favor of my family of orphans, but since that cannot be, then I am grateful that at the least you will not withhold approval of expenditures for them."

"Dursten is another matter. And I warn you that I believe he will not be persuaded so easily as I." His hand, smattered with age spots, fretted at his temple. "Perhaps Sir Harry *did* feel I might be too lenient with you, my dear. The wise course is to put your money to work through investment. Yes, I'm sure I should be advocating investments. Oh, to Hades with it—" He broke off his last, vehement words to rise heavily and lumber over to the windows.

Kerr's usually proud bearing was lost in a sagging body which looked to Lea very much older this day than it had even the day before. He seemed of a sudden burdened to collapse with a weight of worry. And, in a flash of intuition, she knew it wasn't only the pretty kettle of fish with her co-trustee that was troubling the solicitor. Something else was preying on his mind. His practice in London was large, and it was obvious to Lea that she couldn't be his only client with difficulties. There were probably many "Durstens"—and the problems they created—with which he had to contend. She frowned. On the other hand, it might not be business affairs, but poor health that plagued him.

She went to him, placing a gentle hand on his bowed shoulder. "Are you ill? May I get you something—a bromide or tisane?"

He continued to look out the window. "No, no. For what ails me," he said in a strangled voice, "I'm afraid there is no bromide or tisane." He shrugged and with an

84

effort straightened his shoulders, shaking off Lea's hand. When he turned to face her, it was his usual hearty countenance he showed her. "A breath of air. What I need, my dear, is just a breath of fresh air." He wheeled sharply away and left the room hastily.

Mildly surprised, a little disturbed, Lea stood irresolute in the small, formal salon, not knowing whether she should go after Mr. Kerr or let him be. At last she decided there was nothing to be gained by pursuing a man who so obviously wanted to be alone with his thoughts or with his pain. No, there was nothing to be done in that quarter. She chewed at her knuckle as she set her mind to her own needs, revamping her afternoon plans being paramount. Then, with purpose, she walked briskly out into the wide passageway, passed the great hall on her left and went into the narrow corridor that led to the back of the house and the morning room. She went immediately to the rent table. The verse they had found was not on its top, and she hadn't really expected it to be. Her house was well run and one of the servants would have cleaned the room and put the paper away. She began to search the rent table, not just for the clue they had turned up, but for others that might be in the drawers. Their discovery of the one had put a stop to looking for more. She was well into the second drawer with no result when she felt a prickle along her spine. The drawers were not at all in the condition they had been. Someone—Nigel immediately came to mind—had systematically turned out the contents and reordered them, though she'd never known Nigel to be so neat. In a twinkling she knew there would be nothing to find. The tidy little stacks of papers, clips and the like in the drawers looked as arid as the bones of a picked-over carcass. She felt more chilled than angry that Nigel would have done this without mentioning it to her.

Secretiveness was a trait she found most difficult to live with.

A faint sweeping sound along the passageway outside the room came ever more distinctly to her ears, then receded. The prickle along her spine turned into goose-bumps all over her body. In an instant she felt shot-through with annoyance—she wouldn't be the victim of feelings of discomfort in her own home, not from secretly searched drawers nor from a valet walking through her hallways. She marched out. She wanted to meet this Blaecdene who had inspired in the sensible, unimaginative Suderanne a "kind of fear."

Lea's voice stopped the man as he was walking by the entrance to the great hall. "Blaecdene. It is Blaecdene, is it not?"

He turned slowly toward her, bowing acknowledgement politely enough, but without the slightest trace of subservience or humility. How accurately Suderanne had described him, Lea thought. He was framed by the arched doorway to the great hall. A magnificent late-fifteenth-century Flemish Hunt Tapestry, the only antique and valuable tapestry at Gravetide, hung on the far wall of the room behind him. With its enormous figures in vivid colors, the tapestry was a perfect backdrop for the dramatic figure of the valet who looked the very Devil in the flesh. All black. Crisp black hair curled low over his forehead close to thick black brows that almost met to form a heavy slashing line above coal eyes. He wore a formal suit of clothes, extremely old-fashioned for daytime wear, with breeches above stockings and buckled shoes. And every one of those garments was black, down to the midnight silk of his stockings and below to the jet of the buckles on his shoes. Only the narrowest bands of snowy white linen showed at neck and wrists. He dared not glower or speak forbiddingly to her, of course, but she could imagine him doing so and, had she been Suderanne with him behaving in an overbearing way toward her, she thought she might have gone even further in describing him than that good woman had. Sinister. She cocked her head and continued her appraisal, unmindful of the long silence. Yes, sinister would be her description.

"You wanted a word with me, madam?"

She fancied then that his voice was black, too—black satin, soft and slippery.

"Yes," she said slowly, before gathering the force of her thoughts, "I would remind you, Blaecdene, though I'm certain you've already seen for yourself, that Gravetide is not one of the great houses with a multitude of servants such as the ones you and his lordship appear to be accustomed to visiting. We are rather more modest a little household here, and while staff will do all they can to make the stay of your master comfortable, I am afraid they are not up to demands for luxurious treatment. Since his lordship is travelling with such a large entourage, I request you to press some of his servants into fetching the quantities of hot bath water and the like which he requires."

"Your meaning is well taken, madam, and I shall endeavor to see to it that we do not place a strain on your servants."

He bowed and turned to go when her voice again arrested him.

"And, Blaecdene," she said sharply, "I should appreciate an explanation of your presence in this part of the house. What brings you here?"

"My Lord Dursten asked me to seek out the Book Room for him," he answered smoothly. "And to inform him of the contents of your library. He is, sad to say, travelling with few volumes at the moment and is sorely in need of some diverting reading matter."

Her eyes narrowed. "You will inform his lordship,

then, that every room at Gravetide is, to some extent, a Book Room—as undoubtedly your investigation has revealed. Please also call to his attention the shelves lining the wall of the Oak Room directly opposite his bed. They hold many works by Shakespeare, Spenser, Marlowe, Jonson, Bacon, to name but a few, plus a number of classics along with treatises on subjects such as astronomy, geography and mathematics. There are other volumes whose subjects I forget at present. Probably Lord Dursten and you were too fatigued after your journey to notice," she said with a rather smug satisfaction at exposing his empty explanation for nosing about where he had no business. "We *do* try to make certain our visitors are amply provided for—with books, if not servants," she said tartly. "And if nothing in his room is to his taste, Blaecdene," she added, though fearing she might be gilding the lily of her set-down, "do have his lordship see me for directions to more interesting materials."

He thanked her graciously enough, but there was an unreadable emotion in that fierce face as he did so. Respect? Amusement? Irritation? She couldn't tell. As he moved away down the hall, she closed her eyes, listening to the whish of his movement and filling her mind with the sound as if it might brush forever out of her life the valet and his odious master who'd set him sprying on her or her household or both. She screwed her eyes tighter. "Sir Harry, Sir Harry," she whispered fervently, "whatever possessed you to leave me in such a muddle at the mercy of That Man?"

9

Nigel stalked up to Lea in the Entrance Hall where she was rearranging a gardener's stiff bouquet into free, random sprays more in keeping with the natural gaiety of the spring blossoms.

"What the blue blazes is going on around here?" He glared at her as if he held her responsible for a crime against his person. "Someone has been creeping about in my room at the first crack of dawn."

"You look remarkably well rested for one who was so rudely disturbed," she commented airily, refusing to take seriously his propensity for the dramatic.

"Don't patronize me, Lea. This is extremely serious. And, undoubtedly, all your fault. If you didn't treat the servants and every other inferior for fifty miles around as equals, they wouldn't be so uppity as to dare come pilfering in bedchambers the minute a man leaves."

"Leaves? Why, Nigel, I can't believe you were up with the sun. I've never known you to short yourself on sleep except for the routs or balls you tell us you attend elsewhere. Certainly you never do so when you're rusticating in the country with us. Whatever caused you to rouse yourself so early?"

"That is neither here nor there at the moment.

What you should be concerned about is the theft. The clues have been stolen."

Her amusement died. "Clues? There was only one clue you had access to, if I remember rightly, and none you were—"

He interrupted loudly. "For safe-keeping I took the one we found jointly, plus another I'd uncovered from the rent table later." He snuffled, the only betrayal that he might be feeling the least abashed. "Then, after you'd told us all last night about finding the one in the marriage chest, I collected it from the desktop in your room. You'd damned little concern as far as I could see and were willing to have the things scattered about without a thought for their security." He'd paced to the far side of the hall while making his revelation; now he walked rapidly back to face her. "And this theft proves me right."

"Nigel, do get off your high horse with me. I'd scarcely be able to maintain a shred of self-righteousness in this situation if I were you. And don't dare to attack me on issues of thievery and security when you yourself—shall we say, appropriated?—the clues and then lost them! Lost them, I repeat, because you know it is preposterous to make a charge that servants or laborers at Gravetide would steal anything from us, much less a few scraps of paper which would be incomprehensible to them!"

Nigel began to shout over her hot words when the authoritative voice of Lord Dursten silenced them both.

"Quarreling just after breakfast! You sound like siblings . . . or lovers. Most inappropriate for aunt and nephew-by-law." He virtually sneered at Lea before rapping out, "What's been stolen?"

Lea's breath caught in her throat and she barely heard the explanatory words Nigel eagerly poured out

90

to his idol. Here was Dursten reverting to his scornf
treatment of her after giving her hope last night ar
this morning for decent, though chilly and distant, rel
tions between them. Paradoxical, hateful man! If Nige
was a thorn in her side, Dursten was a dagger at he
throat. Such an allusion coming so readily to mind re
vealed to Lea that she was a trifle afraid of him . . . bu
only, she told herself, because he was so different from
any man she'd ever known.

Her experience with the opposite sex was confined
to men vastly older than herself like her husband,
father, Mr. Kerr, the parson—all gentle, thoughtful persons with whom she could share intellectual interests. Or
to the men of the land like Isham Burton—simple,
friendly persons with whom she talked of sowing and
reaping, foaling and calving. Then, of course, there was
Nigel, who fit into neither category. Poor Nigel who as-
pired to be a sophisticate; poor Nigel who was on the
outside of the society he judged to glitter and in which
he wanted desperately to participate. There was so little
to him she thought he just might fit into that world
which, she'd been told, was mostly form with little sub-
stance. But not so Dursten. He did not run shallow. And
he *was* different. What at first had been conjecture was
now confirmed belief after the conversation last evening
and the tour of inspection this morning.

Though ignoring Lea—which she'd told herself was
very much to her liking—Lord Dursten had exerted
himself to be pleasant to everyone else. He'd steered
away from areas of potential conflict to make conversation only on the most general of topics and aspects of
life at Gravetide. He sounded as informed and intelligent as he looked muscular and fit. And he'd surprised Lea. First by accepting Burton into their supper
circle without the slightest trace of snobbery, indeed

appearing to find the steward the best of company. No less had he surprised her when, as they separated for the night and she'd indicated they would meet at first light at the stables for the tour he'd requested, he hadn't batted an eyelash. He seemed remarkably at home with country hours for a man who was said to spend so much of his time in London society.

Then, too, on their tour he'd brought her round to a reluctant admiration for his manner in dealing with Burton and with the workers they had encountered and talked to as they rode about. If she had thought to call his bluff on knowledge of agriculture and dairying, she had been disappointed. He was equally at ease discussing crop rotation, life at court, or literature, it seemed. This recollection stimulated yet another, but one she preferred not to drag to the front of her mind: the curious sensations the man set off in her so that a treacherous part of herself wanted to please and impress him, while a warring faction wanted to alienate him. She pushed away that disquieting response and reminded herself hastily that had he not insulted her and had he treated her with courtesy, still she would have been put off by his gelid reserve. Now, unbridling his nasty tongue once more to suggest she was behaving childishly, or worse, that Nigel might be her lover, Dursten rekindled her furious dislike of him, fanning it to an even greater blaze.

Even as she was grinding her teeth on her anger at him and unmindful of his remarks, she found herself trailing him up the stairs and into Nigel's room.

"Where did you say you'd put them?"

Nigel strode over to a bureau. "Right up here."

"Peculiar you should leave them in such plain view if your object was to safeguard them," Dursten commented.

That was precisely Lea's thought, but for the world

she wouldn't have expressed any support for her enemy. Besides, Nigel looked crestfallen, and she wasn't one for rubbing salt in wounds. "I suppose you didn't think there was anyone who would search in here."

"Certainly not. No one even knew I had collected the clues, much less brought them to my room. Or so I thought . . . wrongly, it seems."

"A hasty conclusion," Dursten said smartly. "We can go into your actions and your motivations later. The point now is to see whether the clues are misplaced in here or if there is any evidence to bear out your assumption they were stolen."

"Perhaps I should call in the maid. She might have put the papers away in a place we wouldn't think to look." Lea surveyed the neatened room with its well-ordered surfaces. Then she noticed Dursten. He, too, had completed a hasty scan and almost at once he went to the fireplace, swept and cold, devoid of logs. On the grate were blackened, charred curls of what appeared to be a parchment. He sifted the fragments through his strong fingers. "Not lost, nor stolen. Destroyed." An edge of a paper had survived and revealed a few loops of writing. He held it out to Lea. One of the clues?"

She knelt beside him and looked at the burnt scrap. "It appears to be." She turned up an astonished face to him. "But who would want to do such a thing?"

"That is more for you to know than me," Dursten said curtly before squinting across the room at Nigel, who'd remained, standing like a statue, beside the bureau. "If you yourself are not responsible for this," Dursten's tone indicated considerable doubt on that score, "then someone must have observed you collecting these papers and taken the first opportunity to get rid of them. Someone in a hurry, I'd say. Any thoughts on the matter?"

Nigel was quite literally on the carpet. He looked

even paler than normal and was obviously at a loss for words.

"It is too much to ask of you, Mr. Carey-Browne, that you give us any *thoughts*?"

"Really, Lord Dursten, a personal attack is not only out of place, but unproductive." Lea was huffy. "And, sir, what we want are facts, not thoughts!"

"Touché," he said softly, a glimmer of a smile drawing the harshness from the lines etched deep between nostrils and mouth. "Difficult to be indignant while on your knees, though, isn't it?" He rose and held out his hand to help Lea up, a hand which, the instant she was steady on her feet, she dropped even quicker than she would the most loathesome garden slug. She looked at Nigel for a long moment, her appearance composed, a thoughtful expression masking her deep anxiety over the turn of events. "The why of this seems fairly obvious—to delay or stop me. The who is another matter. Was anyone about when you took the clues from the morning room or when you entered my bedchamber for that same purpose last night?"

"I already told you I thought no one knew I'd collected them," he said waspishly. "I wouldn't say I was, well, sneaky"—he tested the effect of the word with a glance toward Dursten, but the Earl's face betrayed no reaction—"however, I did have a care to keep the business to myself and do it when no one was near. Of course, I was particularly circumspect when entering your room."

Lea winced. Nigel had tossed off his last remark as casually as if entering her bedchamber circumspectly weren't the exceptional thing. But annoyance on this score served to remind her of Nigel's habitually loose tongue and tendency to boast about the cleverness of anything he originated. She cross-questioned him about to whom he'd talked of his intentions and activities. But she got nowhere as he continued to deny letting slip a word to anyone. Finally, then, exasperated, she said, "This makes no sense. If you told no one and no one saw you collecting the papers, how can you account for them being burned—except by you?"

"My God," Nigel burst out, "you can't think I did it! It's . . . it's preposterous."

"An empty assertion, Mr. Carey-Browne, no matter how vehement, carries little authority. There is a defense for you," Dursten drawled, "if you would only think about the matter as I've been doing."

Nigel looked at him hopefully, but Lea grew vexed as the pause lengthened.

"You seem to find it amusing to tease with this 'defense.' If you know it," she said crossly, "please speak."

Dursten's eyes went wintry over Lea before he snapped his head around to address Nigel again. "You held forth to all assembled last night, and at some length, about your abilities to solve this mystery, had you but a half dozen or so of the clues. You excused yourself disgracefully quickly after Lady Lea told about finding an additional rhyme and leaving it in her room. Someone besides myself undoubtedly noticed and came to a correct conclusion about your aims. Then, I'd guess, that same person saw you leave the house very early this morning and took the opportunity to confirm his surmise. When he—or perhaps I should say she—had done so, the clues were burned. And, as I suggested before, probably in haste or on the spur of the moment."

"Must have been the way it happened—*must* have been," Nigel said heartily and gratefully. But Lea was not so convinced, nor happy with the inescapable conclusion of his theory.

"You imply the culprit was one of the people in the

drawing room last night—Lady Winifred, Mr. Kerr, Isham Burton, even Thomson—all persons I've known for years and trust unreservedly. I can't and won't believe it of any one of them." Her words choked to a stop and the dawning idea in her mind could be read on her face as she looked soberly at her new trustee. Her expression trumpeted: "You are the stranger. You are the one I don't know."

"Much more likely it was one who has the clues committed to memory and no need of them on paper," he rejoined aloud. "Or one who has already absconded with the treasure." He gestured dismissively. "Besides, I have no motive."

"And why should I believe that," she asked fiercely, "any more than you should believe I had no dark reason to burn those papers?"

He lifted one brow in a face otherwise stony with hauteur, daring her to challenge his consequence and authority. That she did and swiftly.

"Look here, Lord Dursten, I know absolutely nothing about you—and more I do not want to know, I might add, except one thing: the reason for Sir Harry's appointment of you as my trustee. It mystifies me. Completely mystifies me."

"No more than it does me," Dursten said coldly. "I should have thought your own husband would have been fathomed always and easily by you."

Nigel, comprehending little of the spoken and unspoken exchange, but reacting to the charged atmosphere swirling between the two, began a feeble attack on behalf of the man he admired. "Now, Lea, you can't possibly mean to cast a suspicion on Lord Dursten, a man of wealth and rank, held in the highest—"

"Nigel, do stop making such an ass of yourself," Lea interrupted hastily and thoughtlessly. "He was the first to cast suspicion on you with the suggestion you might have burned the clues. Think to protect your own interests. And you might start that task by keeping quiet." Oh, she really was discovering in herself a vixenish tongue. And she quite liked it. She wouldn't for the world have stopped herself now and reverted to the "sweet" Lea of old who kept sharp words to herself. She whirled on Dursten.

"We're at an impasse, a flat standoff, whatever you'd like to call it, in our mutual suspicion. To be blunt, it has crossed my mind more than once that you may have had some terrible hold on Sir Harry which forced him to put you into the position of trustee. You obviously consider me treacherous and heaven only knows what else. The only way out I see is to declare a truce during which we work together on the solution of this problem. We may come to trust one another or to have our worst beliefs confirmed. Who knows? But either way, we will make forward progress. What do you think?"

"I think you the most imperious, high-handed, insulting young woman it has been my misfortune to meet." His eyes glinted steel. "However, I agree to a truce. I suppose you have in mind exactly how to proceed?"

"Not exactly, though it is logical to try to retrieve the clues before memory is as cold and withered as those charred papers. In this perhaps you can be of some help, Nigel."

"While I can be none whatsoever."

"If in fact you have never seen any of the clues, then, of course you cannot be."

"We have a truce. I caution you not to forget so soon."

Lea bit her lip, then retorted with humor, "I stand corrected of a grievous slip, my lord Earl." She dimpled in a mock curtsey. "You might be constructively employed in teasing out information about who might have been seen entering Nigel's room this morning." Dursten glowered at her. "H-m-m, I see I offend you once more. It would never do, I suppose, for the Earl of Dursten to behave like an inquiry agent."

"You express my thought, but rather more mildly than I would. No, it would not do." His eyes narrowed. "In fact, I don't know that I want any part of this foolishness. There are more direct and businesslike means to be used in a matter of this kind—means with which you are not acquainted apparently."

"Now it is you who insult me—again."

"I leave you to your games with your nephew-by-law. But don't worry, I shall make sure I am 'constructively employed,' as you put it, though in pursuits far less childish than the clues and inquiries you would play at." He crossed quickly to the door, but paused as his hand touched the knob. He turned back toward Lea, raking her head to foot with scathing eyes. "One more thing, madam. It's easy enough to see you have old Mr. Kerr in your thrall. And your servants, I'm told, coo in honeyed tones about the virtues of their mistress. However, you may stop right now your efforts to beguile *my* servants. It goes without saying that you cannot get 'round me."

The door thudded shut behind him and, as Nigel appeared to be about to burst into speech, Lea lifted a warning finger. "Not a word, Nigel, not one word. I will not waste a single breath on discussion of Lord Dursten."

She couldn't command her own mind as easily as she could command Nigel's silence, however, and the flurry of thoughts that crowded into her brain wasted a good deal of emotion, if not breath. When she had filtered through to Dursten's warning about his servants, Lea realized she must have scored favorably in some way with the valet, Blaecdene, and thus nettled his master. It was with a sparkle in her eye, not a veil of anger, that she returned her attention to Nigel and the problem at hand.

"Now that we're alone why don't you tell me what it was that took you out of your bed so early this morning? That clue I found?"

"Er, well, yes. The Yellow Garden. Even I took the meaning of that little rhyme."

"And you could barely restrain yourself until first light. My heavens, you didn't start digging?" Her eyes widened in horror at the thought of her precious beds and borders savaged by a shovel in Nigel's hand.

"Course not. Weren't any servants available for it. All the stable hands who were up were busy saddling your horses for the tour of the estate, or so they said. Wouldn't dare try to press that fearsome valet of Dursten's into such work. And, then, Burton refused me the help of the gardeners or home farm men."

Lea turned quickly away to hide an irrepressible smile while Nigel continued in complaint of the independence of the workers at Gravetide. So, her garden had been saved because of Nigel's abhorrence of manual labor. More importantly, she'd learned that Isham, Blaecdene and a score of men on the estate at least had seen, if not actually talked, with Nigel this morning. *Au revoir* to his vaunted discretion in the matter. In similar mindless fashion he'd probably blathered the lot of his intentions and activities in the last days to Winifred, Kerr and anyone else within earshot. He'd done so without even realizing, just as she'd surmised a few minutes earlier, but been unable to confirm on direct questioning. Lord, Nigel was such a fool! Her eyes slid over the charred fragments on the grate, and her smile vanished as her thoughts froze. Was he? Was Nigel such a fool? Kerr had pointed the finger at him, then Dursten had, too. Empty-headed she'd always thought him to be, frivolous and shallow in his pursuits, but basically harmless and not without honor. "Callow only," she'd labelled him for Kerr. Could she be wrong? Perhaps Dursten and Kerr with fresh vision had seen more while she was too close to have anything like a true perspective on him. He'd long since finished his critique of the management of Gravetide workers and stood silent, staring at her as if trying to divine her new, probing thoughts about his character.

Through a haze of suspicion she saw him now as canny, canny in affecting the slack jaw, the questioning expression of one too dim or bewildered to be anything but innocent. And, then, true to its mercurial nature, suspicion doubled back on her. She'd always believed she was untainted by Sir Harry's prejudice against his relations. It wasn't so. She *was* tainted. She saw with sudden clarity that she behaved toward Winifred and Nigel little better than Sir Harry had. Condescending. She was condescending with them. Winifred inspired irritation or pity, and Lea stooped, metaphorically, to placate her, never treating her as an equal, as one woman to another. Nigel was irritating also, but a comic figure to her as well, and she snapped at him or teased him as if he were a child. Did they recognize the condescension she had only recognized this moment and resent it? Even hate her for it? Hate her enough to act singly or in league with one another to try to snatch her inheritance? She shuddered. She felt as if her stomach had been wrenched from its proper place and thrust too near her heart.

Hate. It was such an alien in her heretofore snug little emotional world. Her hands clenched into fists, the nails digging hard into her palms. She would shut the door on it, refuse to admit such an ugly creature to her life. Nigel and Winifred *couldn't* hate her. She had conceived such a terrible thing because of this chaos about the clues and the chaos within her—chaos induced by Sir Harry's strange, secret codicil . . . Nigel's intrusions and fueling of her uncertainties . . . Kerr's bad health or state of mind . . . Winifred's more than usual tartness . . . and, most of all, Dursten's disturbing masculine presence and insults, his introduction of incivility and suspicion into Gravetide. There was no hate, no evil loose in her beloved manor, she told herself emphatically. She relaxed her clenched fists. It was all very simple. Nigel was the harmless soul she'd always believed him and was merely up to pranks and hijinks that, somehow, he believed would impress his new-found idol. Something like that, anyway, she convinced herself and immediately sought to prove.

"Of course"—she strove for the most casual tone— "you've been so zealous about the Game that some might wonder, Nigel, but I think I understand. You'd be a hero if you were the one to find the treasure."

"Hero." He savored the word. "I confess I hadn't put it to myself quite that way. Do you really think so, Lea?" He gave her no time for response, but rushed on. "Seemed to me it would be impressive, impressive, indeed. A coup, really." His eyes glistened with visions of himself basking in glories. Lea could almost see his imagined picture of himself receiving the congratulations of all—but especially Dursten—on his diligence and brilliance in unraveling the puzzle.

"And, naturally," his eyes were suddenly back on her, studying her, "you would be grateful. Excessively grateful. I mean——"

101

"Yes. I know. A bit of the blunt to set you up in London."

"Precisely." He smiled broadly.

To appear even more casual and, thereby, to catch Nigel off-guard, she pretended to straighten a small oil portrait of an Asher ancestor, saying over her shoulder, "It enhances your position enormously to win through despite the theft of the clues. I suppose you made a list of them before you burned the ones Sir Harry wrote out."

Nigel's lashless-looking eyes blinked wildly. "Have you gone mad, Lea? I did no such thing because I didn't burn the wretched papers."

"Ah, then those ashes are just to fox us. I really should have guessed." She no longer sought to prove her theory, because in the space of a minute she had become wed to it. "Very well, Nigel, the joke's gone far enough. Just produce the papers and you may crow to the world that Dursten and I—or just I, if you prefer—have been well and truly had on by you."

"Produce them? But I've told you," Nigel said as if stunned, "they've gone. Stolen. Burned. There," he pointed a shaky finger at the fireplace.

Lea's nerves snapped. "You've shown bad taste in humor before, but this is beyond bad—it is execrable. And, it is the end of your interference in this affair unless and until you decide to cooperate by giving me the list you made. Do I make myself clear?"

"But, but, I haven't a list," Nigel stammered. "And you need my help in recalling the clues. I mean you know nothing about the additional one——"

"Enough, Nigel!" With an effort she kept her voice low. "Cooperate or keep out!" And, with that ultimatum she left to go to her own room and try to repair the damage of what she conceived to be Nigel's prank.

Lea pushed away from the little Sheraton desk, rose and stretched out a touch of stiffness in her back. She was pleased at her excellent memory, which had permitted her to record with little difficulty all of Sir Harry's rhymes they'd unearthed to date. Now, what to do with the list? She didn't want to have to go through the exercise of reconstructing it again and, though she didn't believe Nigel would dare pull the same stunt twice, she wasn't taking any chances. He could be a horridly determined character at times. She'd written in very small, careful letters which, in addition to the fact there weren't many clues, meant her list fit on one neat, crisp page. Where to put it?

The sheer curtains fluttering in the light breeze of the lovely spring day caught her eye. Surrounding their filmy sides like sentinels were heavy, stiff brocade draperies. She rolled the parchment into a tight, slim cylinder and stuck it behind the tie-back, only to realize in a flash it would not do as a hiding place. The maid would close the curtains when she came to turn back the bed and prepare the room for the night. She retrieved the parchment, straightened it out and slipped it under the rug. As she bent over, she caught sight of Burton out the window. He was near the gates, pruposefully heading up the winding mile-long drive toward the house. Most likely he needed to see her. She felt a stab of guilt. There was so much to attend to at planting time, and with all the turmoil with Dursten, now this business with Nigel, she knew she was and would be sadly shirking her end of things. She went down to intercept the steward so that he wouldn't have to go to the bother of getting Thomson to fetch her.

"I hope it's not trouble with the planting that brings

you over, Mr. Burton," she called from the front door before taking the steps quickly. "I'd be very happy if it's a simple need for some of Mrs. Runyon's strong tea and good cakes that has drawn you here this beautiful afternoon."

"Not a spot of trouble out and about Gravetide. Rest easy on that score." As was his habit, he turned in profile so that the right side of his face, the unblemished side, was what Lea saw. "Only untoward thing that's happened since I've been back was yesterday when old Ned went over careless with his axe on some kindling and near split his shin in two."

They exchanged the slightly weary, slightly amused glance of two who had experienced together so many of the mishaps of the most accident-prone man within thirty miles. "Some tea, then?" Lea prompted.

Burton shifted his heavy, compact frame. "No, Lady Lea. 'Twas you, actually, I've come to see." He scuffed the toe of his boot in the gravel laying thick in the front drive. "Like I said, there's been no trouble on the estate. But I was thinking you have trouble aplenty in the house, and I'm afraid I maybe added to it."

"You, Isham Burton, add to my troubles? Why you always reduce them by half at least."

His mumbled thanks died in his lapel, and the sound of his toe worrying the gravel scraped louder on Lea's ear. He was transferring his uneasiness to her through that nervous foot and through the force he exerted in pressing cheek and ear into shoulder. Lea had noted soon after first meeting that when Isham Burton was under strain, he pushed his head ever harder downward and to the left as if that port wine stain were the source of his problem and he would crush it.

"I wouldn't want you to think I'm getting above myself as one's suggested to me already," he said with unaccustomed bitterness giving his lips an ugly twist.

Lea stilled her impatience and waited for Burton to explain to her in his own time, in his own way. He was never one for being rushed in speech.

"It would pain me if you was to think that since Sir Harry's not around anymore I've got ideas I can take advantage and lord it over everyone hereabouts."

"I can't conceive of such a thing," she reassured him and waited, waited for his next wrenched-out words.

"Mr. Nigel's the one suggested it," he said flatly, "when I denied him the help of some of our men. They were busy, Lady Lea, or about to be. Was early this morning even before our tour, and unless you told me to the contrary, I couldn't see reason in Mr. Nigel's wanting to take our men off from important work for spading in your Yellow Garden." His eyes slanted toward her and Lea saw curiosity there. "You'd never let him tear into your pretty place, would you? I mean, Mr. Nigel's never been one for the flowers and the bushes."

She exhaled sharply. "Thank heavens you did deny him, Mr. Burton. No, he had no business in my garden nor ordering you about. I'll have a word with him concerning your authority here which he has no right whatsoever to challenge. Is that clear?" She was very angry with Nigel. At twenty-eight he was only a month younger than Isham Burton chronologically, but in maturity he was the junior of the steward by a decade if not more. She bit her lip. "I sounded a bit shrewish just now. Forgive me. It's this infernal . . ." Her voice trailed off.

"I know," he said in a comforting way. "That Dursten's a hard one and—sorry to say it, but you know me for the plainspoken man of the soil I am—he's not too taken with you. I . . . I guess I *have* overstepped my place, because I took the liberty of having a word or two with him on the subject of you."

"You did, did you?" Lea smiled mischievously. "And

105

just what did you say, Mr. Burton?"

He stammered like a boy, his fingers working at the shock of unruly brown hair that tumbled over his forehead, finally saying, "Roundabout like I gave him a few home truths about how things work here, that's all. He's supposed to learn, being he's your trustee, huh?" She thought he looked mischievous, too, through his bashfulness. Then he was serious, as serious as she'd ever seen him. "I've been trying to help in other ways, too. Course with so little book learning, I'm no good at those clues and the like. But I've been nosing around, asking questions. If the Asher . . . er . . . your fortune's here, someone's got to know. Stands to reason that whatever it is it had to be got here—shipped in or such. And if it's hid in your Yellow Garden, it had to be buried. Even if Sir Harry did it all by himself in the dark of night, someone would of noticed something funny. See what I mean?"

Indeed she did see. Burton looked shrewd and proud of his shrewdness and went on in what for him was an exceptional amount of speech.

"Wanted you to know from my own mouth I've been asking questions and poking about. We're too small and close a lot here for anything to stay private, and it occurred to me after Mr. Nigel blistering my hide with his words this morning that some of this might come to your ears and you'd be getting wrong ideas."

"Never that," Lea said. "And I'm grateful for your concern, Mr. Burton."

They parted after a few words on this subject and a brief exchange on the progress of the planting. Lea hoped Burton hadn't noticed her abstraction during the conversation and taken it amiss. She was grateful, not resentful of his effort to help, but she was troubled by the extent of the knowledge about the fortune that

106

might be making the rounds of the neighborhood with unpredictable consequences.

For all his demurs about lack of education, Burton was a quick-witted man, a fact Lea had long appreciated, and his more direct, simple methods might be more productive than hers of playing out the leads in the Game. All very well and good. But "questions" and "poking around"—might they stimulate the involvement of others, well-meaning perhaps, but wearisomely disruptive and underfoot like Nigel?

10

Of course he was a stranger at Gravetide and didn't know the "rule" about not entering her garden when the gate was latched. Still, Lea didn't feel like excusing him as she watched him stride toward her along the lemon-colored brick walkway. The lowering sun was at her back, bathing with last light that great virile figure approaching her. For an instant she trembled like a wind-assaulted, fragile leaf on one of the musk rosebushes whose blossoms would come within a month to bank in ivory petals the fountain and pool near the bench where she sat. Dursten—intruding in her grounds, thrusting his powerful body through the prim perfection of her garden as though he had every right to do so. Her pulses raced. He was dangerous. And not just in the ways she had already perceived, but in some new, inexplicable way that made her want to bolt. Perversely, she did no such thing, but got up and stepped out to meet him.

"No one infringes on my solitude here," she informed him at once, curtly. "Only on matters of the utmost urgency am I ever disturbed in my garden."

He ignored her implied demand for explanation of his presence and looked around. Against her will she followed his gaze, trying to see her Yellow Garden through eyes that had never seen it before. It was spring, but nonetheless there were hundreds of flowers. She and Sir Harry had planned it so that excepting the depths of winter there always would be blossoms in her garden. Her eyes swept from the stand of Leopard's Bane, the earliest yellow daisies, over "Lemon Queen" alyssum, to golden columbine. A few yards to the other side of the pool at their backs was celandine poppy with yellow cushion spurge as border foliage. Later there would be pale yellow wolfbane, tawny foxglove and its brighter yellow sister, and golden larkspur, buttery sothernwood, creamy boltonia. A listing of all the flowers and shrubs would be very long indeed. And how she loved each and every one in that listing and the garden as a whole. It was not nearly so stiff, so formal as was fashionable, and its style, if it could be said to have style, was alpha to omega. In some spots it was orderly to the point of geometric precision, in others it was rustic to the point of fulsomeness. Lord Dursten did not miss either extreme, but he chose to dwell on one.

"Overall a rather chaste bower," he pronounced sardonically. "But here," he flicked a strong finger toward pearly honeysuckle, profuse and running riot over a trellis, "and there," another flick toward cowslip primroses, spilling like melting butter over the edges of their beds, "a betrayal of that carefully contrived image. A trifle of the wanton slips through the facade despite your best effort."

His words whipped scarlet into her cheeks, but all she said in a tight little voice was, "I assume you sought me out here for something other than a backhanded analogy."

Suddenly the full force of his attention, which had been scattered over her garden, was gathered on her, attention so concentrated and fierce that she stepped back as at an unexpected blast from a baking oven. His sensual, slightly cruel lips parted a fraction, but no words came. His eyes—the color of which she decided at this moment was grey, the furious grey of the waters of the Bristol Channel during a violent storm—continued to burn into her. She took a sudden noisy gulp of desperately needed air.

The fabric of her clothing withered away to nothing under his scorching gaze. Instinctively she crossed her arms to shield her breasts against the nakedness she felt every bit as much as if it were fact. For long humiliating moments, but sharply exciting moments, too, she suffered under his ruthless scrutiny. Then, having stripped her, having examined every inch of her flesh, his eyes indolently redressed her—not, she knew, in the soft muslins or lawns to which she was accustomed, but in abrasive wool, scratchy hairhide and every other harsh scourge material his mind could weave.

She was shaken. She could almost feel that hair shirt he had mentally fitted to her bosom, and she turned away from him saying in a voice husky with emotion, "Your opinion of me is very low. You've made that amply clear from the beginning, of course. But I had no idea you wanted to punish me—and for what sins I can't imagine. Certainly the few words and acts of mine you consider insulting and imperious wouldn't be sufficient to warrant the hard punishment you would so dearly like to give."

"Punishment?" His throaty chuckle was anything but amused. "Absurd. You may have noticed I'm no schoolmarm"—the haughty awareness of his maleness lent particular derision to the word—"and, thus, I have no business punishing young women."

She whirled to face him. "Don't try to negate with

every other word what is between. Even if there weren't your words, there were your eyes——"

His hands silenced her, coming down hard on her shoulders to drag her closer. "So it suits you to have it out in plain language, does it? Not even to allow a veneer of civility, of unspoken opinion, to cover our relations?"

She faltered as the wealth of his wrath and contempt washed over her, but it was too late for retreat. She shook off his hurtful hands and with false assurance said, "Of course plain words. No veneer."

"Very well, but remember you virtually demanded this from me." His massive chest swelled with a deep breath. "It galls me to see rewarded for cunning a provocative, scheming female who has ensnared an old man—a buffoon of an old man, perhaps, but kind for all that."

Her eyes went wide with incredulity. "You mean me? Me and Sir Harry?"

"He was an old man, was he not? And you are female, are you not?" Again his scorching look before he answered his own question in a rasp, "Most definitely female—*and provocative!*"

With one startling movement he swooped her off her feet and crushed her against his chest. His hand tore at her hair, pulling back her head so that his lips could reach hers for a mockery of a kiss. She struggled wildly, but futilely against the iron of his hold, against the iron of his jaw bruisingly opening her lips to violate her with his tongue. His left hand, a steel vise holding her head, was in mad contrast to his right, which plundered her soft body with the sensuous deftness of strong, beautiful fingers that had long known how to touch a woman.

He released her as abruptly as he'd pulled her to him so that she reeled and very nearly lost her balance.

Horrified, hurt, she raised trembling fingers to her aching lips. "You beast," she gasped. "You brutal . . . brutal. . . . No one has ever . . . Not ever. . . ." Tears of outrage dammed the flow of words threatening to become utterly incoherent and she spluttered to a halt.

"Not to your liking?" he growled softly. "You prefer something more along these lines?" And, then, still defenseless from shock, she was caught up in his arms again. His lips brushed lightly over and over hers, sipped at the tears raining down her cheeks, nuzzled her ears and throat until her shock turned to anger and her anger to some terrifying kind of thrall.

She was head-to-toe in a vortex of tingling sensation, a vortex that sucked mind and thought into its center to swirl them to bits before spiralling her into a creature that was nothing but sensory body. Vision—a panorama of scarlet from the torrent of blood beneath her closed lids. Smell—the masculine scent of him mingled with the perfumes of the flowers all around. Sound—his hoarse murmurs and her stifled ones over the play of water splashing into the fountain. Taste— sweet and salty of her tears on his lips and of his skin. And, all over, the feel of him, the touch of lips, hands, hard body. A maelstrom of sensuality. She fought her way up and out of it. She had to . . . had to . . . before her self was gone entirely. And, suddenly, they were apart, eyeing one another, breathless both, but with two very different kinds of emotions. She was appalled, he victorious.

"You never got *that* from your fatuous, aging husband, I venture. Where, then?" He looked truly angry and ready to shake her until her teeth chattered. "From that listing, muscular steward of yours?" His eyes narrowed and he asked viciously, "Or does your foppish

113

Nigel have unsuspected talents in these directions?"

Utterly undone, desperate for understanding of what had happened to her, cruelly lashed by his accusations, she could only stare at him with hurt, questioning eyes.

"Ah, very becoming," he jeered, "this going-all-over-innocent act. I assure you, my dear, you are quite effective in making yourself look beautifully lost. But," he added nastily, "you may save your considerable acting skill for another on whom it may work. I am immune to such wiles."

"You came here for this?" she murmured, almost disbelieving. "To abuse me and insult me?" Her voice caught on a sudden sob, and she was no longer caring for herself, but, oddly, for her garden. "You sullied this place," she accused, "this lovely place that has known only tenderness and appreciation and love. You . . . you are a barbarian!"

"And you are a vixen, a grasping one to boot." A strange expression came over his features. "You would try to convince me that this garden, for the most part a pristine one, is an extension of yourself. Sweet Lea. Demure garden. Given your past and what's just transpired between us, you can hardly expect me to credit that. More this garden is what you might like to convince the world you are." His eyes relented slightly. "I will give you this much—that your garden reflects what you were as an innocent child before the mercenary woman sprang forth."

"Sprang forth, indeed." She leapt on his choice of words as if she'd caught him out. "Eve, full-blown out of Adam's side and here to lure you into original sin, I presume. Oh, what a study in warped theology and warped manhood you are! Thank God Sir Harry is in happy oblivion of what he's done. He would die again a hundred agonizing deaths to know he'd chained me to a trustee who was a confirmed misogynist."

"Woman hater?" he snorted. "If you think to indulge in name-calling on that score, think again. There are a dozen beauties in London who could give you vouchers that I am anything but a misogynist."

"I know better. From what I've heard about the falseness of London society, the pretty little minuets danced around the most simple truths, I chance those 'beauties' are as devoid of any real knowledge about you as you are of me. Further, I'd chance not one in that polite company has ever seen you behave as ruthlessly, as primitively as you have just now. Oh, yes, a misogynist you are most definitely—and a more thoroughgoing one I can't imagine." She tossed her head defiantly in the face of the anger he fought to hold back. She'd give as good as she got and she'd never, ever try to explain or defend herself to this monster.

"Doesn't it occur to you," he said in a ferociously low voice, "that I may not dislike women in general, only you in particular?"

She pointed a rigid finger toward the gate. "Please be good enough to leave my garden this instant."

His eyes glittered with suppressed fury, but his mouth curved into a false smile. "Ah, but we get to my real purpose in tracking you here, a purpose you'll be all the more delighted to hear now. Not only will I quit your garden, my dear, but Gravetide as well. I've decided to leave tomorrow afternoon. I have business of my own to tend in London, but it is the arrant nonsense with clues, the theft of clues, the destruction of clues, and the like that has persuaded me London is the better place to work at untangling your affairs."

"Your attentions are scarcely required when there is a respected solicitor like Mr. Kerr——"

Dursten's *sotto voce* oath stopped her cold.

"Is no one exempt from your disdain?" she asked angrily, "even an elderly and distinguished man like Mr. Kerr?"

"As big a fool financially as your husband, if not bigger, and remiss from the beginning in handling this estate."

"A fool financially? What twaddle! He's very well off, a most skillful and astute investor."

He hooted with scorn. "Skillful and astute! Did you not know that the man you praise for those qualities is teetering on ruin?"

Her lashes fluttered over uncomprehending eyes.

"Bankruptcy," he said impatiently. "It is known through all the investment circles in London that your solid Mr. Kerr has plunged heavily and unwisely in shipping stocks and corn futures after disastrous reverses last year in other areas. He's mortgaged to the hilt and near to losing the very cravat at his neck, old-fashioned and frayed though that cravat may be."

An anguished gasp escaped before Lea could stifle it. She did turn in time, however, to hide from Dursten a pained expression. So that was Kerr's burden—loss and debt. Her heart went out to him in his trouble. But why had he not confided it to her? Even asked for help? That she would most assuredly give him any assistance she could he must know with a certainty. She fretted for a few moments before turning back to Dursten, but he had vanished without even the sound of his step on the walkway or the snap of the gate behind him.

With a little cry she ran to the bench on which she'd been sitting when he arrived and composed herself much as she'd been then. If only she could persuade herself that the time between then and now had never passed, that the devastating scenes of passion and hate had not been played out. Appropriate, she thought wryly, that those scenes should have been played out here in this most dramatic spot in her garden.

Entering by the gate at the east end and whether meandering along the pebble-strewn paths or coming more directly along the brick walkway, one couldn't fail to be drawn to the west wall, which bore the focal point of the garden. During the first seven years of the garden's existence, Lea and Sir Harry had tried many things in that spot which they knew should be the focal point, but none of them had really worked. Then Sir Harry had been inspired to build a pond there, a project he undertook with great glee. About a year and a half before his death he'd been further inspired to add a classical statue and fountain. He had been as coy and playful about the whole thing as Lea had ever seen him and delighted in surprising her with the statue. In exquisite opalescent ivory-colored marble, it was of a man peering eternally into the pool at his feet. From a fountain hidden behind him water sprayed over his shoulders and trembled into the pool below. The composition worked perfectly—the new statue and fountain blending beautifully with the old pool, which was oval in shape with a gilt-colored stone basin and facings and edging of tawny marble. A companion slab of the tawny marble formed the bench nearby, placed perfectly for the contemplation of the fountain and pool. It was here she sat.

The tinkling waters should have been soothing as they always had been, but now, serving to remind her of the quickening desire Dursten had aroused in her, they had the opposite effect. She was prickly with nerves. How could she have surrendered her senses to a man she despised and who despised her? Without an answer, she felt her emotions dissolve in a shambles. Tears of anger and bitter regret welled in her eyes before they were overtaken by tears of wild, frustrated desire to annihilate Dursten . . . annihilate him and all that had swept into Gravetide with him.

A horrid memory, long and often repressed, gushed up and would not be stanched. Damnable Dursten. He had taken away her power to cap it as she had always managed to do before. Images of that episode of a little more than two and a half years ago bobbed and churned, on her dread of them. They would not be denied.

It was her wedding night. Dressed in sheer white cambric and lace she trembled, waiting in a huge four-poster for her friend who was her friend no longer, but her husband. The crack of the opening door pierced the romantic gloom from the candles in ornate floor stands that guarded either side of the bed. These candles only, Sir Harry had ordered the chambermaid, were to be lighted. It was not a romantic figure, however, but an aging boy, playful in his embarrassment, who'd poked his head round that door. And it was for Lea a ludicrous spectacle who pushed his way into the room, dressed as of course she'd never seen him before in nightcap and gown that ended abruptly at surprisingly bony and wrinkled knees. His first embrace, rough from awkwardness, made her flinch, and elicited from him exaggerated apologies. His hot breath on her cheek, his soft, almost flabby lips clumsily seeking hers made her shudder. He lurched into even more avid attempts at lovemaking. His passion embarrassed her, then frightened her, then so filled her with repugnance that she pushed him violently away.

Never would Lea forgive herself the misery she had caused Sir Harry that night . . . and after. But, much as it pained her, too, she could not compel herself to allow his touch, much less respond to him. She had been sick

118

with revulsion, revulsion as enormous as if it had been her very own father who had come to her bed to take her virginity. Incest. Consummation of their marriage would have been an act of incest. She had blurted it all out to Sir Harry. And that dear, sweet man, stunned and broken-hearted though he was, had comforted her, vowed he would never force himself on her, assured her that he would still and always love and cherish her. But, those words out, he'd broken and wept at her bosom like a motherless babe until he'd sobbed out his sorrow and had fallen asleep in her arms.

It was the hearty and bluff Sir Harry of old from the next morning on, but occasionally in their succeeding months together she'd caught him looking at her with so much mingled hurt and desire she'd barely been able to stand it. And once, not long before his death, when she had intercepted that look, he had scratched up his nerve and said, wistfully, "If only you were married to a younger man, a man whom you loved, Lea, and who could introduce you to the exquisite passions. You will never know how much I wish that for you."

Repugnance and shame—or was it guilt?—were the twin emotions of that memory which she yearned to blot out of all recollection. So great was her anxiety at experiencing those emotions that she leapt up from the hard bench to pace around it for several minutes before resuming her seat. She'd come to her Yellow Garden to look for a likely hiding place for the treasure or an inspiration as to its nature, but that purpose had fled with Dursten's arrival and she no longer had the capacity for it, absorbed as she was in her emotions. She continued sitting there, and time quickly passed as her thoughts threaded between events long ago past between her and Sir Harry and recently between her and Dursten. With a start she realized the sun had gone down and a stiff chill, unusual for mid-May, had crept into the air. She rose, strangely reluctant to be alone in the dark, and looked toward Gravetide.

The servants had lighted candles throughout the house, their flames dancing invitingly, and yet she felt as reluctant to return as she did to remain in the gloomy garden. She forced herself to move, heading for the gate, but she walked slowly, her normal brisk strides the victim of emotional weariness.

A cool gust caused her to shiver and she paused, wrapping her arms about herself for warmth. It was then she heard the sound—the crunch of a carefully placed foot on the pebble path parallel to the brick walkway she used.

"Who's there?" she called out.

There was no answer. She must have imagined the sound, she thought, and went along.

Crunch. There it was again. The stealthy, but distinct sounds of feet moving across pebbles. Faster now. Closer. And instinct told Lea not to call out again for the identity of that softly, carefully walking person, but to flee. Heart pounding, she raced for the gate, the foot-falls behind her faster and no longer careful. He was gaining on her, near to catching her. She fumbled with the latch. It wouldn't lift. She tore at it, ripping a fingernail off at the quick, scratching and cutting her hands in desperation to claw open the latch. Was it tied down? It had to be. There was no other explanation for its refusal to budge because it had been in perfect condition when she'd come into the garden.

Her pursuer was almost upon her, his breath coming fast and loud now to her ear. Frantic, she lifted her skirts, ran back a few paces, bumping hard into her chaser and knocking him off balance. Then, as she'd done when she was a child and no one was looking, she ran full tilt and jumped the low gate. She stumbled as she landed, but was quickly on her feet, off and running hard for the safety of Gravetide.

11

"Watch out!" Winifred screeched as Lea, having just flown through the back door to the house, almost careered into her in the narrow rear hall. "What have you done, Lea? Your hair! Your face! Why, you're even panting." Winifred regarded her with exactly the censorious expression Lea had seen on a hundred occasions throughout her childhood when, dirty and dishevelled, she had the misfortune to wander into the spinster's view. It was restorative, bracing this throwback behavior of Winifred's and, impulsively, Lea hugged her.

"Well, I'm sure I don't know what *that* was for," Winifred said archly, prodding back into the bun at her nape a lock of hair that had dared to slip out when Lea had embraced her. "What I do know, though, is there's a rip in the hem of your gown. And you appear the same hoydenish child that father of yours and that brother of mine used to encourage to run wild over the countryside." Her features and voice were severe, but Lea thought she detected a softness about the eyes and mouth that hinted at some pleasure derived from the unexpected, unusual hug.

"How does it happen at your age, Lea, that you revert to such scandalous disregard of the proprieties?"

Lea made the instant decision not to put her off as she would have done in the past, but to act in accordance with the insight she had had about her condescending treatment of the older woman and tell her the truth.

"Someone . . . someone was in my garden . . . and gave me quite a fright," Lea said baldly before rushing into an account of what had happened, ending with her leap of the gate and her race for the back door. To her surprise Winifred was neither disapproving nor hysterical. Instead of the display of the vapors she had fully expected, she heard Winifred commenting in a most matter-of-fact tone.

"Undoubtedly one of those thieving vagabonds we have to contend with now and again. You remember just a month or so ago when that tramp was caught with those silver spoons and the two loaves of bread after stealing his way through half the county?"

Lea put up her hand to signal a halt. She certainly did remember, and she shuddered at the recollection of the fate of the man Winifred had called a tramp, but she had considered a poor old fellow, down on his luck. He'd been guilty of pilfering and not of major theft, but he'd been shown no mercy in the courts and had been sentenced to hang. Lea would never accept this cruel "justice" reserved for the poor.

"Then, before, there was that drifter," Winifred resumed. "The one who filched half of Mrs. Runyon's Christmas puddings, cooling on the sills. Last October it was. By the by, if I didn't remark on those puddings, it——"

"You did, you did," Lea interrupted hastily, recalling clearly Winifred's incessant carping. The kitchen had become too busy in the succeeding days, lengthening into weeks, for Mrs. Runyon to get back to making replacement puddings, and when she did have time it was mid-November. Winifred complained throughout the Christmas festivities that the puddings had not been put down long enough and were not nearly as steeped with brandy as they should be.

"We must get to the present situation," Lea said quickly. "This man may be more dangerous than that drifter. . . ." She stopped short. "Whatever could he have expected to steal from me in the garden? I have no purse with me, in fact nothing that would attract a robber."

"You're wearing an extremely valuable chain and locket," Winifred supplied instantly. "Gold fetches a handsome price nowadays."

The frown left Lea's creamy brow. "But of course, Winifred, and how stupid of me not to have thought of that at once." She looked down at her small, slim hands and the two unostentatious rings she wore. "And think how awful if I'd lost Mother's ring! My wedding band, too," she added swiftly.

"My dear," Winifred exclaimed in sudden alarm, "those bloody scratches and your poor nail torn off! You must attend to those hands right away." At a snuffle of resistance from Lea, she hastened to add, "Don't fret for a moment about this problem of the thief. I'll have Mr. Burton alerted immediately. He and the men should take care of this quickly enough. A stranger doesn't get by for long around here, and probably they'll have caught him before another sunset—if he hasn't fled Somerset already, since he must know he's sounded an alarm by going after you." Winifred steered Lea by the elbow along the hallway.

"I'm so glad it was you I ran into and not some other I can think of." Winifred chuckled. A queer sound. If Lea had ever heard it before, she'd failed to note its peculiar tenor. "How was it I was lucky enough to find you in the back hall?" It seemed an unusual place for Winifred to have been at that hour.

"I was just looking out for you, as it happens." Winifred had a frog in her throat. She cleared it noisily. "It's a special night, you know, and I discovered you weren't in your room dressing for supper, and it is well past the hour for us to assemble in the Formal Salon— not that sprawling great hall for once. Well, at any rate, I was concerned and naturally inquired into your where-abouts. Suderanne said she'd last seen you heading off to your garden. I'd checked the morning room first, of course, since you're so often to be found there, and I was just about to go outside and look for you myself when you came barrelling in." Winifred, it appeared, was prepared to go on for minutes in excruciating detail of her odyssey in search of Lea, but they had reached the foot of the stairs and, thus, Lea had an excuse for parting from the chatterbox.

Safe in her room, Lea trembled on the thought of a strange, desperate man wrenching the rings from her fingers, ripping the delicate locket from her throat. She rubbed her neck where it throbbed from the power of her imagination. The hall clock tolled the hour. Late. The others would be gathering in the salon. Mr. Burton and the people around Gravetide would deal with the would-be thief, she reminded herself to force the problem away. She hastened in dressing for the evening.

The large copper tub Suderanne had prepared sat on a hearthrug before a small fire, blazing cheerily to keep a chill from the bath. Dear Suderanne, always an-ticipating her needs, building this fire on a chill night despite the fact it was mid-May. She tested the water. It was still hot, as she'd expected it to be, but it was differ-ent tonight—specially perfumed with her favorite scent, one of the most difficult and expensive scents to make, tuberoses. The fragrance was delightful, but with its aroma came Winifred's words, to which she'd paid no heed at the moments of their utterance: "It is a special night, you know." Oh, dear, yes it was. May 14th. Lea had quite forgotten, though apparently Winifred and Suderanne had not and were seeing to it that her birthday eve would be celebrated as it always had been. Her heart sank. How could she struggle through *without* Sir Harry and *with* Dursten?

The water stung her hands but its heat began to ply away at her tension. She eased neck-deep into its warm fragrance and closed her eyes.

It was twenty-two years ago this night that Lea had come howling into the world just as the clock had finished striking midnight. "You weren't really meant to be an ides child, my darling," her father had told her often. And, later, when she was older and acquainted with the facts about birth, he supplemented that statement with details of her mother's protracted labor. The midwife had been forced to get the assistance of a doctor, and neither could believe that both mother and child had been able to survive into the 15th day of May, even by so little as a minute or two. Perhaps because that night had been such an agony and then an epiphany for him, perhaps because he truly considered the 14th her birthday, or perhaps just from whim, he'd always celebrated it. The party was early when she was tiny out of respect for her bedtime, grew progressively later as she herself grew, and since she was thirteen had culminated at midnight with the presentation of a cake and presents. It had become tradition—a tradition that now, this night, was to be carried on despite the death of its originator and the deaths of all save Lea who had participated from the first.

Into these gloomy thoughts about loss dawned a dazzling one: Dursten would leave tomorrow. A cause for celebration if there ever was one! She shot out of the bath, a sudden merry tune on her lips while she briskly dried her body to a rosy glow. Incredibly relieved and wondrously exhilarated, she dared to select from her wardrobe a canary-colored voile which, after one wearing a year before, she had rejected because of the immodesty of its sheerness and its décolletage. Sir Harry had selected the gown for her and had been effusive in his admiration at her appearance in it, declaring her more lovely that the loveliest lemon lily, a flower he'd so loved that he'd had stands of them massed at each side of the picket fence leading into her garden.

Lea liked the current styles. The empire lines were flattering to her tiny figure, making her look even more fragile while lending her the illusion of a bit of additional height. It was her one concern about her looks that she had not grown more than a couple of inches above five feet. The waistline of her dress, pulled tight beneath her bosom, was a garland of knotted satin ribbon, the only decoration except for the same ribbon threading the low neckline and the edges of the capped, ruched sleeves. She had more of the ribbon for her hair, which she caught up high at the crown into a cascade of lustrous auburn curls.

It was all the rage to deck oneself in a rainbow of colors, a rage Lea couldn't abide and so instead of the peacock blue shawl, the violet slippers, the lime-beaded reticule another might have selected to go with this dress, she chose white accessories. Rarely did she wear gloves, considering them a nuisance, but since her hands marred the perfection of her appearance, she slipped on a dainty wrist-length pair in soft French kid.

Lea twirled before her long mirror. She looked anything but demure and knew a wicked delight in leading Dursten on to an even more outrageously false opinion of her. She knew, too, a momentary, unaccustomed vanity. How lucky she was in her roses-and-cream complexion, she thought. Few women were so untouched by the slightest trace of sallowness that they were able to wear a brilliant drift of sunshine like the one swirling about her.

It was a radiant Lea who moments later crossed the threshold into the formal salon and in time to hear Dursten drily reacting to something Nigel apparently had said. She was aware that Dursten had spotted her coming down the hall and not only intended his remark for her but in all probability conceived it because she would be within earshot.

"Too often," he said, "the children of such deep romantics suffer from disillusionment. It turns them into the most brittle of cynics and as such prone to try to take advantage of the tender emotions in the people they encounter."

The "deep romantic" was her father; the cynic, she, of course. Yet again Dursten had thrown down the gauntlet, and she was not the one to let it lie. Besides, she was honest enough with herself to admit, after her humiliation in the garden it was easier to face him with hot words on her lips instead of memories of his hot kisses there.

"What a sad phenomenon you relate, my Lord," she said from the doorway before gliding smoothly to Nigel's side. Her enormous hazel eyes hadn't left Dursten's face during her progress through the room, and their expression suggested seething resentment and defiance barely held in check. The expression in his eyes thundered his opinion of her alluring costume—that she was, at last, dressed in a fashion appropriate to her character.

"Nigel," she pronounced his name with feigned

chiding, "how naughty of you to induce Lord Dursten into unflattering remarks about his origins, his character, his conduct. Whatever did you say to prompt such self-revelatory talk?"

Behind her she heard Winifred squelch a little gasp of dismay and Mr. Kerr cough softly in embarrassment. There was no response at all from Dursten, but Nigel, indignant though baffled, spoke up at once in his own defense.

"Why I said nothing at all about his lordship! Ain't the done thing to comment on someone's personal affairs or to 'induce' him to do so as you suggested. Right, Dursten?"

"Quite right. But we must forgive Lady Lea," he said with immaculate sarcasm. "She didn't hear the preliminaries, of course, nor does she know her subject. No one familiar with the St. John lines would ever make the mistake of conjoining my family name and the word romantic." He tossed this last off lightly, a faint smile curling his lips, but his eyes were bleak.

In part from his words, in part from those eyes there came to Lea an intuition, an insight perhaps, about Dursten's early life that was so poignant she was compelled to turn away. How austere, how loveless had been the family which had trained into their boy-child those qualities she had abhorred in Dursten from the first. She was suddenly madly curious to know the circumstances which for two summers years ago brought the young Lord Dursten to Gravetide—probably plain Collin Mannings St. John then, as it would have been early to have succeeded to the title. At the first opportunity, Lea noted, she must probe Thomson. Perhaps Winifred, too, might know something.

"I say, Lea, you aren't paying the slightest attention!" Nigel tapped her arm impatiently. "What I'd been trying to tell Lord Dursten before you came in and got us off on a silly by-path was that story about how you came to get your name. Thought it appropriate for your birthday eve and all that. 'Fraid I got the tale a bit squirrelled, though. Those curst Greek legends with their confounded twists and turns."

"Yes, I'm afraid all Dursten could gather," Kerr offered amiably, "was that it was a near thing in your first hours that you'd go through life as 'Hero Ellington,' due to your father's"—he hastily broke off to substitute "classicism" for the contentious "romanticism" that had nearly rolled from his tongue.

"I sincerely doubt Lord Dursten's interest."

"Ah, but I am interested, Lady Lea. 'Leandra Ellington Asher' struck me as an attractive name when I came on it in the will, the Leandra unusual, too." He sounded almost human for a change, but quickly destroyed that impression with his next words. "I should like to know its origin, provided I don't have to coax to get it."

"I thought you believed I never had to be *coaxed* into anything," she parried, before giving it up at the look on Dursten's face. She hurried to get the explanation over and done. "It's a simple story. For a reason I never fully understood my father was quite taken with the legend of the beautiful Hero, a woman so attractive in so many ways as to be able to lure Leander to swim the Hellespont night after night to be with her. The tragic end to the legend didn't impress him sufficiently, it seems, to keep him from wanting to name me 'Hero.'" Her eyes misted. "My father relished telling that it was the one and only time my mother refused him anything. She absolutely put her foot down on having her infant daughter shackled with 'Hero,' but she did suggest the compromise—that they feminize Leander's name—which made father happy enough."

"And the shortened version?" Dursten asked idly.

"From Sir Harry. He said Leandra was too elegant for such a little scrap as I was at four when he first me me. Lea stuck and no one thought to revert to Leandra when I was older."

"I . . . er . . . good evening." Isham Burton was suddenly in their midst and looking painfully bashful. "Forgive me for being late, holding up the party, but it took a bit of doing to round up some folks to look for the man what tried to attack Lady Lea in her garden."

Thomson was just then handing Lea a goblet of champagne from the silver tray he carried. His hand trembled so violently that champagne spilled over the frosty edge of the thick crystal and onto the turkey carpet below.

"Beg pardon," Thomson mumbled, shakily but quickly replacing the casualty on the tray and offering Lea a fresh goblet.

There was a flurry of comment and question from the three gentlemen who were strangers to the information Burton had imparted, and in her concern with responses, Lea dismissed Thomson's unusual clumsiness from her mind. Later she would castigate herself harshly for the oversight and wish fervently she had taken him aside at that instant to ask what was the difficulty.

Throughout supper the subject of the would-be thief or "attacker," as Isham Burton had tagged him, especially titillated Winifred and Nigel, inspiring them to drag out every phrase of gossip and rumor that had ever come to their ears about evil vagabonds and their odious deeds. Mr. Kerr was a bit more interesting in supplying anecdotes about famous criminal cases, but overall the conversation was boring in the extreme to Lea. Dursten and Burton kept silent and lent her no support in her frequent attempts at a change of subject.

Since that first hideous meal, Dursten had been seated properly at her right. Now she leaned toward him trying to start a side conversation that would kill the bird of boredom and the bird of curiosity at a throw. She asked his opinion of how the estate differed now from what he'd found as a guest many years ago. Rude as she knew him to be, she hardly expected the set-down she got.

He hadn't failed to notice, he said, her avidly curious expression after his unfortunate remark about his family. And, he informed her, he had not the slightest intention of satisfying her curiosity as to anything in his past, including as innocuous a topic as Gravetide.

Her eyes flashed, but she managed to curb her tongue and in moments was rewarded with a sweet vindication of her reputation before Dursten. It came from Isham Burton. Though shy personally, he was not at all reticent in matters that had to do with the performance of his duties. He caught Dursten's eye and asked him if he would be good enough to confine members of his entourage to the immediate environs of the manor house.

"There are so many travelling with you, my Lord," Burton explained, "and all of them strangers to the folks hereabouts. Lady Lea is much loved and respected in these parts. I hate to think what would happen to a man of yours if he was mistook for the one that came after Lady Lea. The people around here would tear him limb from limb."

"I shall send out an order through Blaecdene at once to restrict their movements." Dursten said, beckoning Thomson to him and requesting the message be relayed to his valet. Then he added, looking at Lea rather than Burton, "but your fears for my men will be short-lived, because I leave with the first light in the morning." He had returned from the Yellow Garden in a mood of reckless anger. And, had it not been for Blaecdene, who'd put a few soothing but discreet words in his ear, even now he would be engaging in a treacherous night journey over the notoriously pocked and rutted roads in this part of Somerset.

"So, you've moved up your departure time," Lea commented.

"My birthday present to you."

A sparkling ripple of laughter caused all heads to turn in Lea's direction. In a voice for Dursten's ears alone, she rejoined pleasantly, "Jewels, art treasures—they would pall beside your gift, the generosity of which stuns me. I'm indeed grateful, my Lord."

This piece of banter, or perhaps the imminent departure that prompted it, reduced hostilities between the two to the considerably lower level of light sarcasm. Everyone responded to the change and a more pleasant atmosphere prevailed.

On the stroke of the witching hour the baize door opened and house servants and outside workers came trooping through in the wake of Thomson who bore a cake surrounded by candles. There were momentos of the occasion, some wrapped which Lea put by to open on the morrow. Happy returns were called loudly. And Mrs. Runyon and Suderanne took the liberty of kissing Lea on the cheek when they proffered their happy birthday wishes. One young stable hand even ventured a tease about her sadly advanced age. As Lea was sure the lad had been dared—and none too gently—to make the jest and had had to brazen the courage for it, she laughed especially merrily for him.

The workers welcomed this night, she knew, because a barrel of the best ale, wheels of the finest Cheddar Gorge and Gravetide cheeses, and other treats were laid out for them in the Servants' Hall. But simple anticipation of their party could not account for the warmth Lea sensed flowing from them to her. The expressions on their faces, the words of goodwill they offered were so genuinely moving that she found it difficult to make her little speech of thanks after the cake cutting.

Her joy in the moment was abruptly over when it came time for Thomson to give his good wishes and shake her hand—the formality which signalled the end of the workers' appearance in the dining room and the resumption of their own party in the hall. Before speaking his words for all to hear, Thomson asked in a quiet aside if he might have a private interview with her before she turned in, but after the others had retired for the night.

Her deep, sudden frown followed by the hissed "trouble?" made Thomson flinch. There was an expression of such warning on his pinched, grey face that she felt compelled to play a part, forcing her stiff lips into a smile. "By all means see me," she said softly. "I'll be in the little sitting room adjacent to my bedchamber."

The next half hour saw a very distracted Lea. Not even Dursten, a new gleam in his eyes, could lure her to take on any of his bated comments. She barely managed politeness in getting through the toast from Mr. Kerr, the cake eating, the dreary obligatory conversation of such an occasion. And she only became animated again when she judged enough time had elapsed so that civilly she could put a stop to the celebration and bid her goodnights.

Kerr walked with her upstairs. "Now that Dursten's getting out of your hair, I feel free to leave, too, my

135

dear," he told her. "I'll be off tomorrow, though not at dawn like that vigorous specimen." He looked very old and tired, and Lea wanted to tell him she knew of his troubles and wished to help, but she dared not. "Things will settle to normal with the lot of us gone," he paused, "well, almost the lot. If I were you I'd send Nigel packing. He's a troublemaker in his own witless way and always a strain. But, that's perhaps too forward of me to suggest as it's your house."

About to leave her at the door to her room he went stern of a sudden. "You are not to worry yourself about those hidden assets, that fortune. We'll track it out of London through Harry's business connections. And you can be sure that with Dursten plaguing and pestering, the job will be done in double-time."

She kissed his papery cheek. "I'm sure I can trust in you, Mr. Kerr. Sleep well."

Lea dismissed everything from her mind except Thomson's extraordinary request to see her. She went straight through the inside connecting door from her bedchamber to the little sitting room to wait for him. He had bad news for her, of that there was no doubt, and her mind raced from one troublespot on the estate to another. She waited and fretted, waited and fretted. But Thomson never reached her sitting room. He never even climbed the stairs.

12

Gravetide, venerable old dowager of a house that she was, moaned elegantly in the damp chill of deep night. Lea thrust the candlestick she carried to a safe arm's length from her body and drew her fleecy white shawl higher over the wisp of canary-colored voile touching her shoulders. Two chimes of the clock with still no sign of Thomson had propelled her into the inky, drafty corridor.

The flame of the candle flickered wildly. Not a ray of moonlight filtered through the mullioned windows to aid that brave, quavering little flame in its unequal struggle against the pervasive blackness. Never, even as a tiny, highly imaginative child who had just lost her mother, had Lea been afraid of the dark. Now she was suddenly sensitive to the mysteries of the night, the unknown terrors and dangers which could lurk in its ebony depths. The apprehension flooding her was compounded by self-deprecation. Absurd, infantile, she scorned herself, that a grown woman in her own home, every corner of which she knew and loved, should be prey to phantoms of the night imagination. But the apprehension would not be banished. It grew, not quite fear, more a dismal sense of foreboding. And it controlled her movements, making them over-cautious, awkward. The toes of her kid-shod foot inched over the carpet, seeking, at last attaining the first rung of the stairs. She took the steps gingerly.

At the bottom she played the feeble light of her candle over the bannister in search of the newel table which held a many-sprocketed candelabra. She lighted its candles with fingers trembling in haste to remedy the foolish inadequacy of her preparation for this foray. Twelve candles flailed against the dark. Then twelve more from the companion candelabra on the other side of the staircase.

Just as the brightly dancing flames were beginning to dispel her apprehension, a faint groan came to her ears. Her heart lurched and the vagueness of apprehension jelled into the certainty of fear.

"Lady Lea." A voice so frail she could only guess its owner queried her presence and her help in the same thin breath.

Every fibre of her body went taut as her eyes probed the entrance hall, darting into its shadowy corners and alcoves, futilely seeking the one who needed her so badly. Frantic, she lifted a candelabra high, arcing it to bring light to the darkest nooks. Hot tallow spilled onto her bare wrist, but she scarcely felt it.

"Lady Lea." The second ghostly whisper of her name was forlorn, desperately weak. Still she could not locate the place from which it came. Frustration and anxiety brought a prickle of perspiration to her brow. She rounded the newel post and rushed into the hall, swerving just in time to avoid the prone figure on the floor.

"Oh, my God," she rasped out.

Thomson was sprawled over the door jamb, his legs in the dining room, his torso in the hall. The right side of his face was flat to the carpet, his left alarmingly white and slack. She dropped to her knees, setting the candelabra near to examine his face. His mouth hung loose and the one visible eye was so glazed as to appear unseeing. He'd summoned his last reserves of strength to call to her.

"Dear Thomson, dear old fellow," she crooned, "it will be all right now. I'm here and I'll get help."

She couldn't be certain of her instant judgment that he'd suffered a stroke, but she could be certain his nostrils and mouth were pinched and he needed more air. She rose and went around behind his waist, pulling with all her might to roll him over onto his back. She knelt once more, gently raising his head to cradle it in her lap. She decided to fan his face with her hand and eased her fingers from beneath his neck.

She gasped. Her palm was full of blood, clots of it, trembling there and oozing through her fingers. The yellow of her skirt was steadily turning scarlet as a grotesque halo spread larger and larger around Thomson's head. Shock kept her frozen for a second. Then she was all action. She snatched the shawl from her shoulders, wadded it into a thick pad, and jerked up Thomson's head from her lap. The base of his skull was a crimson blur. With her left hand she pressed the makeshift stancher into the wound, with her right she forced back the front of his head, pushing down hard. She dared not move. Thomson was mewing with pain, a tremulous, weak sound that for all the world seemed to Lea a feeble death-knoll. She fought back a sob, shivered with pity at Thomson's agony and whispered words of comfort to him. He needed help, and urgently. There was no way to get it, she knew, but to shout down the house.

"I'm going to call for help," she warned the poor man whom she feared was beyond hearing her now. "Don't be alarmed."

And, suddenly, she was screaming into the night with a loudness of which she'd never dreamed herself capable. Thomson's body hurtled upward in startle reflex at the piercing noise. She had to shift his position and hers to get the wadding back in place before shouting again for help.

Doors opened; muted, questioning voices could be heard in the corridors above and below stairs; the sounds of at least one pair of heavy, running feet drummed on the steps. It wasn't with the least surprise that Lea realized Dursten was the first to reach them and quite ahead of any others. It seemed natural, as though from the first thought of making that cry for help she had expected him to be the one to answer.

"What's happened here?" His question was out even as he was pounding to Lea's side and lowering himself to the floor to feel for Thomson's pulse.

"Some sort of awful accident." Her words were breathless, jerky. "He has a terrible bleeding wound in the back of his head. . . . I can't move. . . . Can't take my shawl away. . . ." Sketchy and inadequate though her words were, Dursten seemed to grasp their meaning, indeed the entire situation immediately. "We must get the doctor at once."

"No need for that," he said firmly. Her wide eyes followed his assured movement to the foot of the staircase, then up to the faint outline of Blaecdene leaning over the bannister.

"We'll need you on the quick," Dursten called up to him. "Bring your bag."

She felt slightly giddy, but her voice came out harsh.

"He needs a real doctor, a surgeon, not some black Lucifer with a sorcerer's bag."

"I've put my life in Blaecdene's hands, and you'd do well to put Thomson's in his, too."

His tone was emphatic enough to still any further protest from her, if not her doubts. She redoubled her concentration in applying pressure to the wound, a task made even more difficult when Dursten insisted Thomson's head had to be elevated. They changed positions, Lea crawling around to the side, though never ceasing to press at forehead and wound, Dursten crouching where she had been to push up and hold Thomson in a sitting position. Lea's left hand was hot and slippery with blood, her arms, her knees, the small of her back ached abominably, yet even when Blaecdene arrived she would not give up her post. It took Dursten with all his strength to wrench her away and roughly drag her aside.

By that time everyone had been drawn to the hall. Directly in Lea's line of vision were the servants up from their rooms on the kitchen level. Next to the staircase wall was Nigel supporting Winifred. Mr. Kerr had posted himself near the dining room. Someone had had the presence to run all the way to the carriage house to rouse Isham Burton whose rooms were above, because he was there, too, standing a few paces down from Nigel and Winifred.

Just as the night time had erased her rationality, it erased class distinctions, too, Lea observed with a fascination for detail born of shock. On this bizarre night even the apparent sex differences were diminished— servant, family member and friend, male and female, looking very much alike. White night gowns were amazingly similar when dimness made it impossible to tell rough cotton from delicate lawn. Robes, hastily donned,

141

rumpled over the limbs, hung so badly from their wearers' frames that the excellence of tailoring or lack of it was lost to the eye. The general frowsiness of sleep, particularly of hair, made Winifred look a sister to Suderanne, to Mrs. Runyon. Only Isham Burton looked different, though she couldn't figure out just how. She was jolted out of the dazed state that provoked these observations by Blaecdene's smooth voice, very soft. If she hadn't been sitting within inches of him, she wouldn't have been able to make out his words. They were chilling in their simplicity, their precision, their consequences.

"He was hit more than once. A large swelling well up on the head. Two gashes at the base of the skull. They're almost contiguous, but definitely separate." Blaecdene's fingers were probing Thomson's wounds, but his eyes were fixed on Dursten who silently acknowledged the information.

Blaecdene shifted his black gaze to Lea, asking a question that for a moment sounded peculiar.

"You had champagne tonight. It was iced?"

She nodded dumbly.

"It was late when you left the dining room and the servants were having a party of their own. The buckets won't have been emptied. Have someone get me anything left. Cold water. And, particularly, any pieces of ice no matter how small."

"Better still," Cook Runyon called out, "if it's ice you need, I've a cold box in the larder with a big hunk in it. I'll chop some pieces off."

"Fine for later, but empty the champagne buckets first," Blaecdene was in full command and terse. "More accessible. Faster. On second thought, just bring the buckets themselves. Speed is essential at this moment."

The cook ran off to do the job and Blaecdene called to Suderanne. "Towels, please, lots of them."

Lea found her voice. "Winifred, the rolls of linen bandages in my kit in the morning room."

"That won't be necessary," Blaecdene said. "I have bandages in my bag."

"Winifred," Lea said peremptorily and over-loud, "Please hurry to get those bandages." She felt a sudden urgency to break up that ragged circle of peering faces, to dispatch them with speed away from the airless, grim little area in which Thomson lay mortally hurt. She caught Dursten's expression. He seemed to read—or share—her thought. In a shaky voice she could barely recognize as her own, she heard herself ordering Kerr, Nigel, Burton, the maids to a variety of tasks. Then she was back between Blaecdene and Dursten, watching and assisting when she could in the application of icy cold towels, the bathing, stitching up and bandaging. Ice wrapped in towels, was packed around the back of Thomson's head. While Blaecdene was rubbing brandy on the patient's lips, gently but firmly patting and pinching his cheeks in an attempt to bring him back to consciousness, Dursten pulled Lea to her feet and took her aside.

"You won't want the sickroom to be out of the way," he said meaningly. "The room you directed that little maid to prepare a few moments ago, it's upstairs?"

"Across from mine."

"Good. Any other access than through the one door in the hall?"

Her "no" brought a satisfied grunt, and he moved away abruptly to prowl the hall before disappearing into the dining room. Lea kneaded her fingertips into the hollows at her temples on sudden throbbing pain. She pushed harder at those tender spots and squeezed her eyes shut. She *couldn't* let herself think about the meaning, the understanding that prompted Dursten's questions. She couldn't think about that until later, after the crisis was past.

One by one all those she'd sent on errands drifted back to the hall. Candles had been lighted at her direction, and the brighter light heightened the drawn, shocked faces hovering a few decent paces back from the deathly pale Thomson. Not a word was spoken, not even a murmur escaped the dozen or more people standing vigil there. The breathless waiting for a sign of life from Thomson, the silence through which fluttered Blaecdene's steady, gentle slaps to those pallid cheeks was a nightmare of suspended time. When Lea could bear it no longer, she ran back to Thomson's side, took his cold, flaccid hand into her warm grasp and began to talk to him. She said anything that came to mind— reminiscences of childhood adventures in which he had a part, tales Sir Harry had told of his loyalty and devotion. And interspersed through all were pleas for him to open his eyes, to try to regain consciousness.

Whether it was her urgings, the brandy, the slaps, Lea would never know or care—she would remember only the joy of seeing Thomson's heavily veined, puffy lids flutter, then his eyes open, unfocused at first, gradually recovering intelligence and finally recognizing her. He stiffened his abused head, trying to raise it and was gently restrained by Blaecdene. A croak came from his parched lips.

"May I give him water?" Lea asked the valet, whose competence had impressed her to such an extent that she respected him as much as any skilled physician.

"Please do. He needs as much fluid now as he possibly can take. The blood loss, you know."

Someone thrust a cup into her hand, and Lea held it to Thomson's lips. But after one deep gulp, he refused more. His eyes were feverish on Lea. His hand in hers tightened in a deathlock grip, and his mouth worked violently at speech that would not come.

"Don't, don't," Lea cried. "You mustn't try to speak. It's too much for you."

Thomson's eyes held desperation. His mouth twisted with effort. Suddenly in a harsh choking voice came the words he had been frantic to produce.

"*Fidus Achates*" reverberated dully through the hall.

Suderanne let out a loud sob. "Saints Patrick and Mary protect us!" she said before bursting into uncontrollable weeping and being led out of hearing.

Thomson's hand released Lea's, then gripped hard again.

"*Fidus Achates*" grated from his tortured throat once more.

Lea was stunned and fighting to keep from dissolving into tears as had Suderanne at the words. "And you have ever been my faithful friend, too, Thomson," she whispered. "And Sir Harry's faithful friend, of course. Yes, yes, our *Fidus Achates*." Tenderness and horror mingled to almost take her breath away, and her tone was fierce when she was able to add, "But you are not going to die! Do you hear me, Thomson? You are not going to die!"

There was a violent, shuddering twist to his head as if he'd tried to shake it in negation and then his eyes closed once more. Blaecdene pressed Nigel and Burton to help move Thomson to the bed that had been prepared for him. When Lea started to accompany them upstairs, Balecdene firmly ordered her away, urging her to take some brandy or wine and let him see to the nursing of Thomson in the next critical hours.

Strong arms propelled Lea from the staircase and in the direction of the formal salon. She was like a sleepwalker and, as if from a long distance away, she heard herself saying forcefully, "No. No. The morning room. I want to be in my morning room." The salon was passed, she was into the room of her choice and being shoved into a deep wing-back chair. Soon a brandy glass was pressed to her lips, the fiery liquid it held bringing her sharply to her senses. Winifred was talking—to whom? Lea looked around to find Dursten, Kerr, Burton and Nigel watching Winifred closely as she explained the drama and the shock of Thomson's words.

"It's no wonder Suderanne took on and Lea was thrown into this state," Winifred said in a high, slightly hysterical tone. "'Fidus Achates' were Sir Harry's last words, his deathbed words, and they were spoken to Lea while her hands held his. The scene was so much like this one with Thomson that I . . . well . . . I shudder at the whole thing. I was there at the end with Harry, of course, so was Suderanne and so was Thomson. We all saw it."

"Fidus Achates," Lea repeated. Her leaden voice had a will of its own and droned out as if repeating a school lesson. "Achates was devoted to Aeneas, the mythical hero of Troy and Rome, the son of the goddess Aphrodite. It was about two years ago when I became really interested in Virgil's Aeneid. Oh, I'd read it before of course, but for some reason it wasn't until I was almost twenty that I truly appreciated the work and got deeply involved in its study. Sir Harry teased me about my scholarship of a 'paid piece of writing.' He said it was all whitewash and glorification because Virgil had written it for his patron Augustus whose family liked to claim descent from Aeneas. But really Sir Harry was pleased. He was always pleased with my enthusiasms. He talked of

146

buying me a present to commemorate my study on the *Aeneid,* but I guess he forgot, as I did until this minute. . . ." She looked lost as if searching for the thread in her tangled words. "*Fidus Achates.* The great friend and loyal comrade of Aeneas. His name is proverbial for a trusty friend."

She looked from face to face. Would no one say something? Ask her to tell more of Achates and Aeneas? Anything to prolong this time, this theme so she could delay thinking about Thomson's eerie use of Sir Harry's last words?

She sniffed the brandy as if it were smelling salts and put up her free hand to shield her eyes. She didn't want to deal with the horror of what had happened to Thomson or her responsibility for it. She felt crushed with guilt. What if she had not waited so long to come looking for him? What if she had lighted two dozen candles, not one, and come thundering, not creeping, down the stairs? She would have warded off the attack. She would have spared Thomson the vicious assault that might mean his death.

And then a new and even more terrible suspicion entered her mind. She was to blame. Actually to blame. Because she had given Thomson away in the dining room when he asked for a special interview! She remembered his quick look of warning, and the memory made her gasp. The beast who had struck down Thomson was no outsider, but one of their own! One of the persons assembled in the dining room. A person who was desperate to prevent Thomson from talking to her. The same person who only hours earlier had stalked her in the garden?

She lifted her stunned, tormented face and looked directly up into Dursten's knowing eyes. Sometime during her agony of revelation these past few moments he

147

had crossed to stand in front of her, using his body to block her from view of the others arranged on the far side of the room. He took the brandy glass from her limp, bloodstained hand.

"There wasn't much you could have done to prevent what happened to Thomson—not at this stage." His voice was soft but not kind. "Snap out of it, Lea. We can discuss all this after you've bathed and rested. You've had enough for one night, and you don't want to sit around in this dress any longer than you have to, I'm sure."

Vacantly she looked down. Her skirt was soaked all the way up to the garland of satin ribbon beneath her bosom with Thomson's blood, the tiny capped sleeves spattered with it, her arms and hands stained. She wanted to scream and rage that she would see to it Thomson's attacker had to be covered with this bloody garment, feel the sticky warmth of those vital fluids he had spilled wantonly. But all she said and so low it was a whistled breath of barely audible words, was, "Whoever he is, he will be made to pay dearly for what he's done this night."

13

From a writhing half-sleep in no way soothing or restorative, Lea shot up full awake and damning herself for the softness, for the stupid trust which had allowed her to take to her bed these three hours and more. She had no reason to exempt Dursten and his valet from the wariness with which she knew now she must regard everyone at Gravetide. At best it had been weak-minded, at worst a symptom of having lost her wits entirely to have let that pair take over as she had. She couldn't believe truly that either had any part in the assault, but then she couldn't believe truly that anyone she knew might have done such a heinous thing. Logic dictated that suspecting no single one of the crime, she had to suspect every single one of it and act accordingly. First and foremost was continuing protection of Thomson. How *could* she have abandoned him?

She battled free of the twisted bedcovers that had been captive and capturer of her limbs, grabbed for her dressing gown and sailed toward the sickroom. She didn't know exactly what her tingling nerves and disturbed mind were leading her to expect behind that closed door—the sinister-looking Blaecdene meticulously slicing Thomson's vulnerable throat?—but she certainly wasn't prepared for the scene that met her eye. So silent was she in entering the hushed room that not even a click of the doorknob betrayed her arrival. Her breath came out in a gushing sigh of relief at the tableau she beheld. Across the bed from Blaecdene was Suderanne—and if she couldn't trust the woman who'd fussed over her like a brood hen since she was four years old, then there wasn't a soul in the world she could trust. Cook Runyon had pulled up a chair behind Suderanne. Isham Burton was a solitary post at the foot of the bed, and Mr. Kerr nodded in the dim corner behind Blaecdene, who couldn't look less sinister at the moment. The attitude of his body, bent over the absolutely still Thomson, was more than solicitous and concerned, it was positively maternal.

Suderanne caught sight of her, tiptoed to her side and motioned her out to the hall where they could talk. "He's in a bad way, our Thomson. 'Touch and go,' Blaecdene calls his condition, says he's in a coma and his pulse is real weak and thready." She swallowed hard, pressing her thin lips so tight they disappeared into a fine, straight line. It took a moment until she was able to go on. "Sorry I went to pieces like I did in the hall, but I got a grip on meself right soon and rushed up here even as I saw you being led into the morning room. Haven't let Thomson out of sight for a second and I don't intend to more'n I have to. Cook's come up to spell me for a couple hours."

"What's your opinion of Blaecdene?" Lea's brows knit. "Has he been giving herbs or other medicines to Thomson?"

"Nairy a thing, save water and I've poured that out of the pitcher." The lines around her eyes crinkled with the keen look she gave Lea. "Can't say I've decided to like that devil in black, but I can't fault his nursing, not so fars, anyway, and I'm not feared of him like I was at the first."

"And Mr. Kerr and Mr. Burton have been here the whole time?"

"Well, not the whole time, but most of it. I swear that room was like a mill at threshing time for the first hour with the two in there now, Lady Winifred and Mr. Nigel, even his lordship himself coming and going, coming and going. Pretty soon Blaecdene lays down the law and tells them one and all that they stays or leaves, but they can't be traipsing back and forth making commotion and drafts and such-like."

"Good for Blaecdene," Lea said, but she kept the rest of her thought to herself. There was safety in numbers all right, but danger in the confusion of their movements. Could Blaecdene really be on their side and have called a halt to those entrances and exits because he anticipated that danger? She gave Suderanne a gentle push. "You're a dear, good woman, and you should be off now for your couple of hours of rest." As the maid lingered, Lea asked in swift concern, "Is there something more? There hasn't been other trouble?"

"Now, we've had trouble enough for one night," Suderanne answered evasively.

"Oh, please, please don't hold back on me. I can tell you are, and we can't afford anything but openness between us." Her voice was shrill with urgency.

"Deary, deary," Suderanne said, alarmed. "I'd no idea you'd fret yourself in such a way. It's nothing for you to get riled about. I've on my mind a little thing Cook told me, that's all. They had quite a scene in the kitchen with young Anna. But it's not for you to worry. Mrs. Runyon thinks the girl just wanted a spot of attention and that's why she was carrying on with her tale of a ghost and how she was leaving Gravetide because it was haunted. All a lot of superstitious piddle, you see? They've got Anna all calmed down now and agreeing to stay. So I wasn't holding nothing back from you really."

"It was Anna I sent up to prepare the room for Thomson, wasn't it?"

Suderanne nodded. "And it's then she thinks she heard the ghost. The ghost of Sir Harry, she says, come back to his bedchamber, thunderous upset and stalking around in there." She patted Lea's hand. "But you know, she only let out with this tale after she'd heard about how Thomson's words down there was Sir Harry's last words. So you can't set no store by her. Like Cook said it was probably feeling left out and being nervish. We're all nervish."

But Lea was not so prepared to dismiss the girl's story as the product of a fevered imagination or a bid for attention. Anna had always appeared too steady and self-effacing for either explanation to hold. Seizing Suderanne's hand in a rough clasp, she said, "Come with me. I think this needs looking into." They hurried through the little sitting room where Lea had waited in vain for Thomson. It lay between her bedchamber and Sir Harry's, which had been closed since his death. The door was ajar, the room within a shambles.

"Dear Lord Almighty," Suderanne exclaimed as the extent of the havoc came home to her. Lea said nothing at all. Dust covers had been snatched from the furniture and lay in spectral heaps about the room. Drawers, clothes press, chests had been emptied and their contents scattered. The linen had been ripped from the bed. Partially dragged off the frame, the mattress rested at a precarious tilt, its stuffing popping out of a dozen slits along its length.

Lea forced herself to wade through the destruction. "A frenzied search, but thorough," she pronounced.

Candle wax was everywhere. She pointed it out to Suderanne. "We're lucky the wicked vandal didn't start a fire and burn the house to the ground." But after this effort at normalcy, her breath started to come raspy. It wasn't the thick dust that choked her. It was the additional qualities of the attacker of Thomson revealed by his ransacking of the bedchamber that almost took her breath away. To the savagery he'd displayed in the assault on Thomson were added by his carnage of the room cunning determination and daring. Especially daring—for, while his victim lay below and people had been dispersed to tasks throughout the house, even to the preparation of a room across the hall, he had had the boldness to rip Sir Harry's bedchamber to pieces. *And he'd got by with it!* The audacity of it, the success of that audacity were bitter as bile—all the more bitter, Lea raged inwardly, because of her impotence. How could she retaliate or even see to the punishment of an unknown villain? All at once she felt the utter necessity of separating herself from this viciously plundered place. She bolted into the sitting room. Suderanne was at her heels and, while Lea paced and wrung her hands, the maid began a litany of "I knew it. I just knew it." It finally penetrated and pulled Lea up sharp.

"Knew what?"

"That something was going to happen. You could feel it in the very air, like a great ugly monster of a bird hovering over Gravetide. And all because of Sir Harry's fool playing around." She sank onto a chair. "But even up 'til a minute ago I was trying to convince myself it weren't so—" she let out a sound that was between a sob and a moan "—and that it weren't one of ours what did that terrible thing to Thomson. 'No, Suderanne,' I kept saying to myself, 'it was an outsider, some old sneak thief drifting through our part of the country, thinking to steal a mite of silver and then running amuck when he bumped into Thomson.' Oh, Miss Lea, it all fit together so nice in my head, 'specially because everyone was talking at the party about how Lady Winifred had called out Isham Burton and the men since you was near robbed in your garden yesterday evening." She turned up a mournful face. "But, no, my little one, it ain't so, none of that I've been telling myself. This tearing up of Sir Harry's room proves what I felt in my bones all along. It's one gone crazed for that hid-away fortune who's up to all this evil business."

"Still it could be one remote from us." With eyes closed against the pain of betrayal by one trusted and near, Lea expressed her last hope. "One of the stable hands or home farm men who really isn't close to us at all. An enemy of Sir Harry's or someone who bore a grudge against me." Before she uttered the words, she knew them to be absurd. Her despairing eyes flew open to search Suderanne's face and in its desolate expression was an echoing disbelief of what she had just said.

The older woman shook her head. "It's a puzzle why it was poor old Thomson that was went after. The only think I can figure is he knew something straight from Sir Harry he never told a soul. They was thick in a quiet-like way from the days they was boys together. Everyone in these parts knows that, and someone might have tried to wheedle, then beat out of Thomson whatever it was he had from Sir Harry."

"Or Thomson may have seen or heard something he thought I should know." She ran over to kneel before Suderanne and, much as she had done as a child, to place her head on that capacious lap. "I fear it's my fault he was hurt. He asked to speak to me privately and I gave him away. In the dining room last night. My expression. My—" She cried. It was the first time she had allowed herself to do so in front of another person in years.

"There, there, you can't blame yourself." Suderanne stroked Lea's tangled auburn locks. "If there was no evil on the loose, then nothing bad would've befell Thomson. And you're not responsible for the evil. Remember the story you told me when you was little about that Pandora and her box. Well, Sir Harry set this up real good and proper for a person here amongst us to be a regular Pandora's box of evil with greed busting his lid off." Her hands tightened on Lea's shoulders. "Have a care for yourself. Look what near happened in your garden." She relaxed and added warmly, "And remember you've no reason for faultin' yourself for any of what's been going on."

"Except I should have anticipated the dangers of having a fortune lying around. I should have worked night and day to find it, Suderanne."

"I expect maybe that's so, but there's been a lot on your mind having nothing to do with fortunes. And especially lately when in blows that Lord Dursten to discombobulate you and everybody else around. You've never had the likes of him to contend with before. Such a cold and arrogant one is he, but a real man nonetheless."

Already Lea was regretting her lapse from self-reliance, her need for comfort. She dried her eyes and hastened to her feet. Most of all, she had no tolerance for listening to anything further Suderanne might have to say about the "real man," as she'd termed Dursten. It was those extraneous thoughts about him that had preoccupied her to the exclusion of what was really important, those extraneous feelings for him that had blinded, deafened, numbed her to the dangers at Gravetide. She could afford no more of that.

"I'd better get dressed and see to breakfast for everyone, Suderanne. All our routines will have been knocked out of kilter, and yet the basics of life must go on. And you need your rest now." She steered her to the hall door, stopped, and said in a low, intimate tone, "Promise to tell me anything out of the ordinary you notice these next hours and days. Between us, we must make certain Thomson is watched closely so no further harm can come to him."

Suderanne nodded grimly. "That's for sure—no further harm from foe or erstwhile friend." The words reverberated in Lea's mind as she stepped into a dress plucked randomly from the wardrobe. The words clamored at her nerves as she brushed her hair and tied it back with a band in an uncaring, girlish fashion. "Erstwhile friend" suggested more to her fertile brain than the simple meaning that the unknown perpetrator was and had been masquerading at Gravetide as a friend to someone, if not herself. The words inspired the idea of a conspiracy between Thomson and another to steal the fortune. If Thomson had experienced a failure of nerve or a crisis of conscience and told his abettor of his intention to make a clean breast of it, that person might well have determined to silence him before he could reach her. What basis had she for such a conjecture? Absolutely none. But there was that strange sensation she had experienced during the disastrous first dinner with Dursten when she'd observed Thomson's uncanny perfection as a servant. And what motive would he have for betrayal after a lifetime of loyalty? That question gave her not a moment's pause for answer. Sir Harry was notoriously stingy with everyone save herself—and with her his generosity was so lavish as to be embarrassing. She wished she could remember the look on Thomson's face at the will reading, remember if he'd displayed even the slightest trace of disappointment at the modest pension Sir Harry had designated as reward for his lifelong service. Lea couldn't fault him if he felt entitled to more for all those years of devotion.

But who would join him or whom would he choose as a conspirator? She sucked in her breath at the sudden image of Thomson and Kerr in deep conversation in the entrance hall the day of the thunderstorm. She'd thought the old solicitor had looked guilty—discomfitted anyway—as he caught sight of her. And Kerr's motive for participation in a scheme to steal the fortune would be crystal clear now that Dursten had made known to her the bankruptcy, the virtual ruin that threatened him. If Sir Harry had had even an inkling of Kerr's unwise investments, it would have been sufficient cause for appointment of a co-trustee to protect her interests. Sir Harry was so suspicious of human nature in matters of money that it would have been typical of his shrewdness in such a situation to have sought out Dursten, a man of assured wealth and rank, to stand guardian . . . just in case.

Pat as her analysis was, it had flaws, Lea realized. First, the brutality of the attack on Thomson did not seem to jibe with Mr. Kerr's personality, though it could be reasoned away on grounds of desperation. It was really the ransacking of the room that argued against Kerr. Even if he had the boldness for it, which she very much doubted, he didn't have the strength within that portly, aging frame, or so it seemed to her.

The breakfast gong startled her and drove her from her room. It was with not a little surprise that she found Winifred reigning over a dining room in which were posted half a dozen male servants, two of whom stood ready to serve from the sideboard covered with silver dishes. A footman escorted Lea to the table and seated

157

her. The azure and scarlet livery of the servants, the abundance and aroma of the breakfast blared usurpation of the running of Gravetide by Dursten's staff—at their master's command, of course. She bit back a stinging rebuke of Winifred for allowing such a thing to come to pass, merely nodded a good morning in her direction, and vowed to herself she would behave graciously toward Dursten for his "generosity."

"Oh, I say, this is capital, absolutely capital," Nigel said by way of announcing his presence at the sideboard, where he was peeking beneath lids at the dishes presented there. "These Frenchie chefs really know their business! And I for one can't wait to dig in." He strode toward his place and enjoyed the attentions of the footman who seated him, flourished a napkin into his lap, and fussed over the angle and depth of the chair.

"So you do not forget your stomach even at a time like this," Lea said archly.

Winifred, marching forward from the rear door, where she'd been in thrall at her regnancy over the many-servanted room, defended her darling in astringent tones. "Wise he is, too. Nigel always keeps his head and has a care for his health. We must all take a lesson from him. We need our strength with a vagabond running about on the loose, breaking into the house, attacking anyone who moves in the night."

Lea looked up from the fruit compote that was being presented by a footman. "It's not such a person who's responsible for what happened to Thomson," she said calmly. "I'm afraid, Winifred, that your theory won't wash."

"No, it won't wash," Dursten repeated, briskly crossing the room with Kerr and Burton in his wake.

The three together produced in Lea a tremor of alarm. "Who's watching Thomson?"

"Blaecdene, of course." Dursten's eyes dared her for

a moment. "And that gorgon you call Cook."

"Anna, too," Burton supplied. "She came in to sit with Mrs. Runyon right before we left."

Lea's nod of assent and relief was lost in the movement of the men to their places. Dursten spoke as he was seated.

"The theory of an outsider doing that job on Thomson won't wash for many reasons, Lady Winifred. Not the least of them is that I found the weapon used for the assault on the dining room floor last night, and it is not an object that someone unfamiliar with the house would have known about or been able to spot in the pitch of night."

"What—" Lea swallowed hard. "What was it?"

"A vermeil candlestick. The base was used as the cudgel. It was covered with hair and blood."

Winifred and Lea turned as one to stare at the now empty side table near the door where the vermeil candlestick had always stood. While Lea was thinking that he had been alert in remembering to search for the weapon in the midst of all the confusion, Dursten launched a new topic.

"I'm made to understand you have some officers of the law in this little backwater. Kerr is advocating we call them in. Burton and I are of a different persuasion."

Burton put his arguments out quickly. "I was reminding Mr. Kerr that the constable is fair weak in the head, the sheriff nothing more than the scapegrace nephew of the Justice of the Peace and as for him, well, that Justice would like nothing better than a chance to muddy Sir Harry's name since they feuded for years over everything under the sun, but 'specially those passels of land near the north boundary."

"You've ticked them off quite accurately, Mr. Burton," Lea said.

"Still and all, my dear," Kerr said, "when an assault

has occurred, one is obliged to notify the authorities."

"They'd clutter up the place and be terrible underfoot," Burton said.

"It's for you to decide, Lady Lea," Dursten added swiftly. "You know these people, while I do not. If they're as poorly equipped for their duties as Burton says, and you seem to support him in his view, then it would be foolish to burden us with them. On the other hand, you might be well advised by Mr. Kerr to follow the letter of the law. Which will it be—call them in or not?"

"A good question," Lea temporized. "But I must thank you for making your servants——"

"I'm not ready for a change of subject yet," Dursten broke into her words of appreciation. "Besides, you're reaching. I know every well you resent like hell my intrusion in your household affairs. However, as I intend to stay until matters are cleared, I refuse to be at the mercy of your limited staff in their attempts at muddling through. My chef was idle, my other servants, too. They exist to see to my comforts and, therefore, they will do so. If others benefit from those comforts provided for me, that's as it may be. Now, about the decision on the authorities . . ."

"Selfish on top of arrogant and rude," Lea muttered under breath while her words, as well as Dursten's, were overridden by Kerr's.

"And I, too, shall stay on until such time as Thomson recovers and can tell us who attacked him or his attacker is discovered by other means." He glared at Dursten. "I wouldn't dream of leaving Lea under the circumstances."

Dursten ignored him. "A decision, if you please," he demanded of Lea.

She looked from one face to another. Perhaps it was

her new-born suspicion of Kerr or Burton's persuasive reminder of the shortcomings of the local men of the law that decided her. "No authorities," she blurted. "I don't want people gossiping from one end of Somerset to the other about the 'sad' state of affairs at Gravetide. For myself I don't care. But Sir Harry would have hated it. Anyway, I don't think the gentlemen in question could help in the least."

"Right of you to decide with his lordship, Lea," Nigel commented. He looked pointedly at Burton. "What we don't need around here is another oaf or three snarling the work of those of us who are serious about resolving this mystery. Brings me to a point, too. Aunt and I were talking about Thomson's use of Sir Harry's last words. Uncommon odd that, don't you think?" He turned toward Dursten and finding no response there, shifted to Lea, who was still smarting from having to agree with Dursten on not calling in the authorities and scarcely listening to Nigel. However, in looking away from her autocratic trustee and to Nigel, she caught out Winifred in an attempt to attract her nephew's attention with a rapid flick of the hand, a moue, and a slight shake of the head urging silence. A chill crawled along Lea's backbone and with it an eagerness to know what Nigel was about to say that Winifred did not want her to hear.

"Yes, it was uncommon odd, and clever of you to perceive it. What do you make of it?"

If Nigel had seen Winifred's warning, he would not heed it, or could not after Lea's appeal to his vanity.

"Well, it gave me a regular brainfever, I must say. Couldn't sleep a wink until, at last, I fathomed it." He paused for dramatic effect. "Thomson and Sir Harry were trying to give you a deep lead on the treasure, Lea. Too easy to pass off '*Fidus Achates*' as sentimental

161

deathbed claptrap. It niggled at my old grey matter 'til out popped the 'faithful friend' in that first clue we unearthed together. You remember—'a faithful friend is a strong defense'. . . and however the dickens it went on."

"And he that hath found such an one hath found a treasure," Lea supplied.

"Now you see? See how the 'faithful friend' in that quotation dovetails with Sir Harry and Thomson repeating *'Fidus Achates'*? You told us last night that Roman chap's name was proverbial for trusty friend. And you kept palavering to Thomson about how he was right he was your faithful friend, Sir Harry's faithful friend."

"Nigel!" Lea exclaimed in wonder. "I do see and you really *have* hit on something." She was genuinely impressed, but surprised and fleetingly dismayed at her underestimation of Nigel who at this moment couldn't restrain a throaty laugh of pride and triumph. Flushed with excitement, Lea leaned toward him. She was on fire to pursue the point, but it was a fire quenched before she could get out a word.

"You will of course mull on this in private," Dursten told her sternly, forcefully reminding her and everyone else at the table that suspicion attached to each of them, as well as to any within earshot of what was discussed in the dining room. It was a reminder that particularly struck hard at Lea, accustomed to forthrightness and open discussion.

Silence of mutual suspicion, generalized suspicion, total suspicion blanketed the room. Long minutes passed. There was only the sound of chairs creaking as first one, then another shifted uncomfortably. Then the squeak of Winifred's fork on her plate played a tune on tight—drawn nerves. Over and over she pulled tines across the film of food she imagined on the china until

Nigel's hand snatched away the fork. Glances meant to be surreptitious were intercepted, the parties looking away instantly. Eyes stumbled to plates, silverware, anything but other eyes. The silence stretched on.

Lea's teeth dragged at her lower lip, her gaze travelling warily over those collected at her table; each one of them seemed more suspicious to her in the minatory silence. Kerr's and Burton's faces were haggard, the younger man's especially and unexpectedly so. Whereas Kerr was ashen, Burton was the charcoal of burned wood. Unshaven, his stubble of beard on sun-browned skin gave it a bluish-black cast which was repeated above leathery cheeks in heavy circles beneath the eyes. Winifred was more rabbity than ever, her moist eyes weepy, nose and pale sandy brows twitching. Only Dursten looked as always—remote and well-groomed and as though nothing had passed in the night except a sound sleep. Nigel, deflated that the sharing of his insight about *"Fidus Achates"* had netted him nothing but this tense silence, was sulky. Lea had an urge to rap out at him for his vain and shallow concern with only himself. Her teeth dug harder into her lip. Nigel appeared to be devoid of feeling for anyone but himself, all right, and it was that lack of grief for his uncle or pity and concern for Thomson which gave him the mental ease to dwell on the strange coincidence of their usage of the same words and find a meaning in it. Her own intense feelings, Lea discovered, were impediments to her now.

Burton's tired voice defied the silence at last. "Don't think I've had a chance yet to tell you, Lady Lea, how bad it makes me feel to see your birthday come up so miserable. I'm real sorry about that. Just look at those presents all around your place. Sad and droopy sight. Don't guess you've a mind to open them now."

"But she must," Nigel said crossly. "Anything for a diversion from this tedious quiet." He shot a quick look at Dursten. "Unless you would think it unseemly."

"I'm hardly a social arbiter," Dursten drawled. "But I shouldn't bother with such nonsense if I were Lady Lea."

She had decided she hadn't the heart for opening gifts until Dursten's comment. He made her feel so contrary. "Of course I'll open them. Why put it off?" She waved at a footman to remove her untoucned plate of food, then scooped the presents from around the edges of her place into a mound before her.

There were the usual numbers of embroidered handkerchiefs from the women in and around Gravetide, some pressed flowers with laboriously copied verses and other similar homemade momentos. Kerr had given her a delicate little gold pin which she knew now he couldn't afford, and it made her heart contract with anxiety. From Burton there was a handsome and much-needed new riding crop. She was sure there would be nothing from Dursten. And, though it was in the pile, she wouldn't get to open Winifred's and Nigel's joint gift for some time to come because of the present she spied next. It was unusually flat, had no name of a giver on it, and piqued her curiosity. It was more an envelope than a package, and she opened it with less care than she had the others, slitting the cheap brown paper with a table knife.

Lea's face crumpled in puzzlement at what lay before her. The opened paper revealed a map of England torn jaggedly out of her own precious altas, which had been a gift from her father. The map bore two crude, greasy marks of an X within a circle over the cities of London and Bath.

Dursten pulled the map away and studied the marks. "What the devil is this?"

And then Lea saw it. The note which had lain beneath the map. Printed in block letters as crude as the marks on the map, the message read:

"Don't be middling smart. Be real smart. Go away. Go to London or go to Bath. But leave Gravetide until the one the fortune really belongs to can search it out. If you don't go, you'll be sorry—more sorry than Thomson."

Lea's fingers trembled, and the note fluttered from her hand to be picked up by Kerr at her immediate left. He read it aloud. Striking her ear with an even more menacing quality than they'd struck her eye, the words caused her body to shake with outrage and fear.

14

Thomson's pale face was so like a death mask that Lea alternately imposed over his quite different features those of her father and those of Sir Harry when their last breaths had escaped them. She was sitting by his bedside now as she had most of the time since running from the breakfast table after discovery of the warning note. There had been no question that she would follow the outrageous direction to run contained in that outrageous message.

Though outwardly she faced the threat with anger, inwardly she quailed, more from shock than fear. She was simply incredulous at that warning of violence directed against her. She—who never in her life had known so much as a hand raised against her in anger; who never had received a reprimand more severe than one of Winifred's vinegary lectures; who never had experienced hostile words or actions . . . until Dursten had come—was totally unprepared for the possibility of personal violence. Dursten's contempt had jarred her, his anger had shaken her, his punishing kisses had enraged her and his sensual ones had catapulted her into a bewildering arena of feelings. But, based as Dursten's opinion of her was on totally false assumptions about her relationship with Sir Harry which she judged to derive mainly from the disparity in their ages, it did not penetrate to her innermost self. The threat of violence did. Dursten was so open in his animosity that she couldn't credit him with the authorship of that sly, serpentine note of warning, much less a dastardly attack on Thomson from the rear or a furtive stalking of her in the garden. But if not Dursten, then who? It was the most haunting, frightening question she had ever addressed.

Lea had left Thomson for only the briefest intervals when necessity to accomplish some task had forced her to do so or when Suderanne had hounded her away to get some rest. Thus, the last twenty-four hours had passed in a blurr of fatigue and trance-like compulsion to protect herself and Thomson and to do everything within her power to unmask the pretender who threatened every aspect of the way of life she held dear. And the last twenty-four hours had passed, too, in a haze of waiting. Just as everyone else did—and especially, Lea imagined, the unknown assailant—she waited for Thomson either to die or to rouse from his coma and speak. The sickroom had become the hub around which pivoted everything and everyone at Gravetide for, since Nigel's deduction about *"Fidus Achates,"* they all believed Thomson to be crucial to the solution of many mysteries. At any time, momentous words could issue from his bluish lips . . . or they could be stilled forever.

Bursts of frenzied activity, both physical and mental, mingled with Lea's waiting. She had sought out Nigel and, much as it irritated her to do so, both apologized for her misapprehensions about the burning of the clues and cajoled him out of the sulks into discussing the one he'd found which she had never seen. His fuzzy recollection of Sir Harry's rhyme had been characteristic of his unclear thinking and imprecise speech. Still it made her wonder if in this instance it was not typical, but deliberate. However, they had got somewhere and Lea believed she had another clue, although at present it didn't seem to help.

"There was some gibberish first off," Nigel had told her of the verse, "about a Second Book of Moses and how it recounted the escape of the Israelites from bondage. It was followed by a bit about admonishments with Sir Harry putting in 'And straw I did not give, but the lordly wealth.' Now *that* I remember distinctly and what came next because it seemed central to the search. Bring anything to mind yet?"

"So far only that he was pointing to the Book of Exodus. The 'lordly wealth' doesn't stimulate any associations at all," she'd told him honestly. "Do get to that next part you recall well."

"Hm-m-m. That was curious. He said, 'Count the leaders.' He gave five Hebrew names I'd never in a thousand years be able to list. After was 'Then count the days of—' and there was a word, Lea, that was *very* peculiar. Never have seen it before. I'll have to spell it out for you. P-e-s-a-c-h."

"Yes, yes," she'd said impatiently. "Pesach. It's the celebration of the most stirring and important event in Jewish history, the Exodus."

In time and after several false starts, the *five* Hebrew names and the *seven* days of Pesach, or Passover, as some called the commemoration of the flight from Egypt and the deliverance, had led Lea to Exodus 5:7— "Ye shall no more give the people straw to make brick." What Sir Harry had said about "and straw I did not give, but the lordly wealth" confirmed they had followed out the lead properly. But for all that, she couldn't help feeling they had lost a great deal by the burning of the clue and Nigel's inexactitude in remembering it.

Immediately, then, Lea had added the quotation from Exodus to the list retrieved from beneath the edge of the rug in her bedroom. She copied the list half a dozen times and passed out the duplicates to Dursten, Kerr, Nigel, Winifred, Burton. She even posted one in the servants' hall for all to see. When she'd tacked that copy to the wall she had said in a ringing voice, "Let the person who thinks he has a right to the fortune find it fair and square from these clues without resorting to any more violence or destruction."

The bedside vigil had provided ample time for her bursts of mental activity, too. She'd thought hard about the warning note and what it might reveal of its author. It was so inelegantly phrased and printed that it suggested a servant or a man with a simple education like Burton. But, then, wouldn't a clever person of polished diction and excellent penmanship have fabricated just such a misleading document? And who, save a deranged person, could possibly believe himself the "one the fortune really belongs to?" The phrase pointed too directly at Nigel and Winifred for consideration unless . . . Her thoughts on these subjects had chased themselves too much for profit, as had her ruminations on the clues. Most of all she dwelt on "Fidus Achates." But nothing would come. Then "Meditate with the Roman, part-named by your favorite hue" would run over and over in her mind next to other clues and the new one, "Ye shall no more give the people straw to make brick . . . and straw I did not give, but the lordly wealth." Her brain was fogged with phrases.

What of Blaecdene's state of mind? He had left the bedside even less than she, but seemed to be bearing the grueling ordeal better, at least in the observable physical sense. Vacillating wildly in her feelings for that black-visaged stranger, Lea would experience confidence in him at one moment, fear of him the next. He appeared a healer and a help, but he could be a partner with Dursten in seeking another chance to attack Thomson— this time successfully—or to silence him should he come around and try to speak to her. Of a sudden that notion seemed so queer and unlikely, so foreign that she wondered if she could perceive anything clearly now. Had she, for example, made any proper sense of the conversation Mr. Kerr had initiated with her a few hours past? Or was her mind hopelessly mired and muddled?

She had flinched when Kerr, following her out of the sickroom, had suggested they take a walk together before she rested. She was frightened to be alone with him . . . or anyone else . . . and rejected his attempts at persuasion in an awkward manner which left him little doubt as to her feelings. Thus, the conversation Kerr wished to have with her was held, as most of her conversations had been these past hours, in whispers just outside the door behind which Thomson fought for his life.

The strain was telling on the old solicitor. Anger and wariness fought for control of his voice. "It crushes me, Lea, that after all these years you fail to trust me sufficiently to allow yourself to be alone with me, especially when you permit Dursten to run roughshod over the household."

"I permit him nothing. He's arrogated control and, frankly, it matters not one wit to me at the moment. Let his chef slave over the ranges. Let his footmen run their legs off serving everyone here. When this nightmare is past I will resume as head of this house. On that you can count, Mr. Kerr."

"If you can wrest back control. All of this may fit into some plan that man has. Dursten's almost a complete mystery figure and I can't tell you how many times I've wondered if he blackmailed Sir Harry into naming him co-trustee."

In that moment Lea knew she had outgrown the unequal relationship that had existed between the young woman and the solicitor, nearly forty years her senior. She no longer took pains to couch her thoughts on a bed of respect but spoke plainly. "You are in the thick of things in London. Why wonder and do nothing when you could have checked on your 'mystery figure'?"

"I did check," he said, stricken by her tone. "And I'm not making idle insinuations as your words imply, but speaking of a fact. Years ago, when Dursten was a young man of about nineteen or twenty, his father divorced his mother. The bill in Parliament was a sensation. Created a scandal that didn't blow over for at least two years. After that time the family seems to have clamped a quietus over their affairs. Nothing much has been known about them from that day to this."

"So that's why he was sent here to Gravetide those two summers," Lea muttered half to herself. "To escape the scandal. And he would speak deprecatingly of our corner of Somerset as a 'little backwater,' when he ought to call it a blessed haven."

"A haven for him those years past, perhaps, but how does he think of Gravetide now?"

Lea clucked in exasperation and Kerr went on talking as if he hadn't noticed her reaction, but he did veer to a new tack.

"Certainly isn't a haven for Lady Winifred. Not with Nigel going at her. Why does that boy torment her so?"

Lea's eyes flew wide. "Torment?"

"They were having a set-to when I entered the dining room for supper. Nigel was goading his Aunt about how undoubtedly everyone here had some small secret

172

he or she didn't want scrutinized. He suggested her little secret might be the nastiest, the most embarrassing of them all. She was crying." Kerr's chin wagged from side to side. "Her sobs were pitiful, Lea, and I can tell you I gave that wretched lad a reading out for his cruelties. But what's it all about?"

"I don't know, Mr. Kerr, and I don't want to know unless Winifred herself wishes to tell me. Sir Harry said there had been a terribly distressing episode in Winifred's girlhood that she was desperate to keep private. It seemed so wrong, then, for Sir Harry to tell me about it that I never would let him. It's all from the long ago and faraway and should be forgotten. If necessary, I will speak to Nigel myself and tell him that if I learn of his continuing on the theme with Winifred, I will throw him out!"

"How like stone you're becoming, Lea. Don't let this business change you so, my dear."

She shook off the hand he'd placed on her shoulder. "It may be I should have grown harder—more forceful, anyway—and long ago," she said enigmatically. "It may be I should have examined your activities with a much colder eye, Mr. Kerr. How bad is this financial mess you're in?"

He shuddered. "Dursten told you, of course."

"Of course," she snapped. "It seems you two are fond of carrying tales about one another. But let's not stray from the point. How bad?"

"Not so bad that it has made me lose my honor, if that's what you're thinking. But it is bad." He averted his eyes. "I didn't want you, anyone to know. So humiliating. And with this business of Sir Harry's capital missing, suspicious, too, I admit."

"All the more suspicious because you kept it dark. If only you'd confided in me!"

He shook his head wearily. "Perhaps I was seeing you still as that youngster ranging free over the estate who shouldn't be burdened. More likely it was my vanity. I failed miserably in my own investments, and I've failed miserably in handling Harry's affairs. Should have rapped him hard and taken the reins. Dursten was right about my folly there."

The situation was so desperate that Lea felt no sympathy at hearing Kerr's tardy confession and no compunction in pressing him further. She pushed her own luck, though, by intimating more knowledge than she possessed. "I venture Thomson knew about your losses, as well as many other things. You shouldn't have gone after him as you did."

"Sweet Lord! You're not suggesting I cracked his skull! No, never. I did try to coerce him—but with words, Lea, with words. I wanted him to share information with me. You came upon us one day in the front hall when I was attempting to persuade Thomson to rely on me, to trust in me. This attack on him supports my hypothesis that he knew a great deal. Harry never could go it alone, as you must remember surely. He was like a very young person who needed a bosom friend to share every little triumph and every little problem. Besides, he would have needed help with the conversion of his capital, then with secreting and maintaining it. He was never one for tiresome details or menial errands. When I discovered you had not been the confidant, the help-mate in this instance, I suspected it had to have been Thomson."

Responsive chords vibrated in Lea. How right Mr. Kerr was about the menial work, the details, the necessity Sir Harry felt always to have someone with him for any and every activity, no matter how small. He couldn't contain his enthusiasms and disappointments, and he

174

couldn't abide being alone in anything. "If not you, Mr. Kerr, then who did this terrible thing to Thomson?"

A baffled expression filled his eyes. "Not only the attack, but the ransacking of the room, the attempt on you in the garden, that warning note—all so vulgar. Despite the vulgarity, however, I would look to Dursten. And most assuredly, Lea, I would call in the authorities as I urged earlier."

"No outsiders," she said fiercely. It had been almost a last gasp, because a stupefying weariness had suddenly overtaken her.

Thinking back on that conversation, she couldn't decide if it made Kerr appear less guilty or more so. Suspicion licking at him, licking at everyone, was a horror in and of itself that made her yearn violently for a time when she could trust unreservedly again, when she could be happy at Gravetide.

Would it ever be possible?

Lea's thoughts roamed back to her father. When her mother died he had found it impossible to go on as before, living in the same house, treading the same streets, seeing the friends they had shared. Julian Ellington's marriage in 1793 to Anne Barrow-Leigh had been a love match and, instead of waning, their fascination with each other had grown every one of their years together. When Lea's mother died of typhus, her father buckled under the grief. His surroundings, so evocative of the loved one he'd lost, became intolerable. And that was why—after a chance encounter with Sir Harry, an old school chum who was a fervent booster of the beauties of Somerset—he had brought Lea to the little cottage at the edge of the Gravetide estate where she'd grown up. He'd had to reorder completely his existence to do so, giving up his seat in classics at Cambridge, arranging an adjunct role translating and reviewing manuscripts.

But, despite a much reduced income and professional isolation, he'd told Lea he'd never rued his decision. Should she, too, Lea asked herself, think about an extraordinary life change? Not now, of course. She'd never flee in the face of a threat or a challenge and not until and unless this horrible business was settled. But after . . . should she? Gravetide might be associated forever in her mind with this grim episode. The thought made her unbearably sad. She had always loved the house and the land so deeply.

She sighed. The house wasn't even hers anymore. Kerr was right in saying Dursten had taken over. His minions swarmed through the corridors and rooms— cleaning, fetching, running errands, doing she knew not what. She couldn't even poke her head through a doorway without butting into one of his footmen, and wherever she went she caught sight of azure and scarlet, colorful shadows to her every move. But even her formidable trustee, for all that he'd assumed command, was not complete master here. Fear was.

The release of the doorknob, though faint and careful, acted like the sudden clang of a fire bell on Lea's raw nerves. Starting up, then subsiding against the back of her chair, she watched Burton enter the sickroom. As always, he walked heavily and decisively. He had told her he was leaving for a hasty meal, and now he was returning to the position at the foot of the bed which had been his from the first. He would stand there for hours, just as she sat for hours, leaving only when she left, if then. Until this moment she'd been grateful for his protective watchfulness, believing that he considered himself to be guarding her and Thomson. But the room was quite full. Too full. Cook was there and Kerr, too. Lady Winifred sat behind Blaecdene showing an uncharacteristic anxiety to contribute to the nursing of the patient. As much a snob as her nephew, Lady Winifred had never shown the slightest inclination to have anything to do with staff, much less to succor them. Burton was not needed in this hushed, stuffy room, but it came to Lea in a flash, he must be needed in a hundred different places on the estate at this their busiest season. Her temper flared. How dare Burton—for whatever good but misguided reasons—contribute to the deterioration of even that most solid, most enduring part of their lives—the lands and herds!

Before she had time to think, she was on her feet, tugging Burton by the sleeve out into the hallway.

"You've hung about the house quite enough, Isham Burton," she told him flat with no preliminaries. Her eyes sparkled with anger, her words were hot and lacking an iota of care for the steward's feelings. "What of the planting? What of the calving and foaling? Who is attending to the business you're so sadly neglecting? Answer me that!"

Lea wasn't prepared for Burton's equally fiery emotion. "So you would slap me back down into what you consider my 'place,' just like Lady Winifred wants to do every time she lays eyes on me, just like her precious nephew tries to do every chance he gets!" But after these few bitter words, he seemed to get a grip on himself or at least to win control over his tongue. In seconds his face spoke of deep hurt and he grumbled, "I wouldn't have thought it of you, Lady Lea." His head, which for a moment had been erect, lurched hard to the left and downward. The sheer pressure he exerted of jowl to shoulder made Lea wince. She felt a pang of remorse at the lack of tact in her words, but not their thrust and tried to tell him as much, concluding her little speech with a challenging question. "Do you want Dursten and his people taking over the farming and the

177

herds, too?" For answer he wheeled and pounded away down the corridor.

"A bit hard on him, weren't you?" Dursten's voice thudded softly at her back.

She didn't turn, forcing him to move around to face her. Her eyes were closed and she said wearily, "So you heard all that. First you set Blaecdene to spy on me and my household and now when he's busy, you do your dirty work yourself, eh?"

He was about to respond and cuttingly, too, she imagined, but was stopped by the door of her bedchamber being flung open. Suderanne, who was using a truckle bed set up next to Lea's, virtually fell into the hall and onto them.

"My God, my God, he's done it again," she croaked.

Lea gasped. "Who's hurt?"

The maid shook her head violently. "Ain't no one's been attacked. It's your room's been searched. More gentle-like than Sir Harry's, but searched. Things are every which-a-way."

Dursten pushed his way past the two women and into the midst of strewn books, gowns, lingerie, bric-a-brac.

"Well searched," he commented before frowning hard at Suderanne. "How could this happen?"

"You mean with me here?" Suderanne asked. "Well, I wasn't here. I come up the back stairs from having a bite to eat in the serving pantry. Saw Miss Lea was dressing down Isham and thought better of it than to barge into them. So I slipped through the door to the sitting room. I just found this mess this instant." Suderanne had come close to Lea to encircle her with protective arms. "You must make certain of my little lady's safety, your Lordship. That warning note to her! Now this! What would've happened been she to come in here when that cur was skulking around. He'd of killed her for sure. Oh, I fear sorely for my Miss Lea," she wailed.

Unaccountably annoyed, Lea shook off Suderanne's embrace. "Have a care to whom you would entrust me. After all, you're looking at a man quite powerful enough to have bashed in Thomson's head with ease, to have pillaged Sir Harry's room so savagely. He was in the hall just now. He heard what I told Mr. Burton. Who's to say he hadn't just come from pulling my room apart in this detestable way?"

"You must admit, though, Lady Lea," Dursten said with a tinge of amusement in his voice, "crude warning notes are quite out of my style."

"A suspicious man, Suderanne," Lea continued undaunted, "a stranger to us and one who claims as his 'valet' a man who seems to me a superior physician."

"Blaecdene does have an uncommon talent for healing. A good deal of training, too, both here and on the Continent—before the war of course."

"And you would try to pass him off as your valet?" It was more a statement of scorn than a question.

"Suppose that Blaecdene did set out his shingle for the practice of medicine, who do you think would consult him?"

Lea's eyebrows winged in a questioning face.

"His infirmity, his countenance," Dursten answered impatiently. "Even you who would like to think yourself above such superficialities called him a 'black Lucifer with a sorcerer's bag' before you'd seen his skill. And that skill you saw only when dire emergency impelled you to use him."

"Dire emergency *and* your domineering ways," she corrected angrily.

"That's true. I am used to commanding. And, simply to satisfy a trifle of that consuming curiosity of

179

yours, compounded by an absurd suspicion of me, it was during the beginning of the Peninsular War that I encountered Blaecdene. We were both in the expeditionary force for the Campaign in Portugal. Later he was assigned as surgeon to my regiment, and we saw action all the way from the beginning until early in 1814. Six years in battle together makes staunch comrades of two men initially well disposed toward one another. In the military Blaecdene could use his talents; in private life he could not. For that reason I kept him with me ever after. He valets me, but he is also physician to the people in my party and, when we are on one of my estates to the people there, too. Blaecdene is too valuable a man to let sink in a remorseless world."

Lea was trapped and held by the grim, bitter lines etched in his handsome face. "You really believe that last, don't you? For you the world is merciless, peopled with the cold and pitiless."

He snorted. "This is hardly the time to delve into my philosophy of life, Lady Lea. We had better stick to the issue which, I recall, was raised by your sensible maid. I agree with her that your protection is paramount now."

"Well, that is rather a surprise to hear from you," Lea snapped. "How is it that you do not accuse me of silencing Thomson so that he couldn't inform you about the manner in which I was squandering Sir Harry's fortune?"

In two swift strides, Dursten had crossed to take her by the shoulders and shake her until her teeth rattled. "I hadn't thought you such a fool! Will you persist in baiting me? And by so doing turn aside from the real dangers here?" He pushed her to arm's length and mocked her cruelly. "Pretty little Lea dandled on the knee of her adoring father, then her doting Sir Harry. Darling little

Lea dancing through her quaint all-yellow garden. Get out of that daze. Behave like a woman—not some golden child whose sharp tongue brings her no consequences; not some shining intellectual presence floating through a crisis of assault and theft as if protected within an aureole."

She had gone limp under his shaking. Now her body went rigid. "Aureole," she repeated numbly. "Aurelius. Marcus Aurelius—a Roman whose second name is from the Latin root for golden, a hue of yellow, my favorite color."

For a moment Dursten looked at her as if she were mad, then remembering the list of clues she'd given him, his eyes shone with the same light of understanding as hers.

"Without a doubt," Lea cried, "we'll find a passage in Aurelius' 'Meditations' marked for us by Sir Harry. He adored the 'Meditations,' always keeping the book close for bedtime reading." She flitted away, through the sitting room, and into Sir Harry's bedchamber which had been tidied, but not restored. The books, carefully housed in shelves on the bed wall before the ransacking, were stacked on the floor and dressers. Lea threw open the curtain to admit light and, noticing that Dursten and Suderanne had followed her, demanded they help her look for the volume.

Dursten found it. The corner of one page was folded back, and a passage on it was marked heavily with ink. And so it was in Dursten's vibrant voice that Lea heard the lines Sir Harry had wanted her to find:

> " 'Look beneath the surface;
> Let not the several quality of a thing
> nor its worth escape thee.' "

15

"Look beneath the surface," Lea repeated, wringing her
hands in anguish. "So, I must have my beautiful garden
destroyed with digging after all. I'd hoped against hope
that we'd find some clue pinpointing the exact location
of the treasure." She sat down heavily on Sir Harry's
bed, burying her face in her hands. "I'm ashamed of
myself. Deeply ashamed. What kind of person am I to
give a moment's thought to saving my garden when it
might be a matter of saving someone's life? It seems an
eternity, not just three days, since I came up with that
clue confirming the treasure was in the Yellow Garden.
Why didn't I turn out an army of men to dig the whole
of it right there and then? That was what Nigel wanted
to do. If only, if only——"

"Stop it!" Suderanne thundered. "The times is
topsy-turvy here and holding my piece ain't worth a
twopenny damn, like the Duke of Wellington's supposed
to say. I won't have you abusin' yourself and taking on
about how you're responsible for everything under the
sun around this place." She whirled on Dursten. "And
you keep your opinions to yourself, Sir, until such time
as you know what you're talking about. Yes, my Miss Lea
was dandled on the knees of her daddy and Sir Harry,

and yes they thought she was the sun, moon, and stars, as we all did and still do. But everyone's mistook who thinks she had a childhood out of a fairystory book. From the time she was ever so wee she was caring for them two old men all wrapped up in their books and their highfalutin jabbering. Never went to a ball, never had friends her age, much less a young man to come courtin', never had nothing but the worry of them two she looked after like *she* was the mother and *them* the children." She turned back to Lea, her ferocity undiminished. "You'll *not* berate yourself for caring about your garden nor for what you haven't done. I won't put up with such talk. You ought to be real good and mad. Mad at Sir Harry—first for heaping on your shoulders every particle of the work to be done hereabouts from the time you was little more than a child. Mad at him, too, for all this tomfoolery he's left you with. Most of all, you should be mad at the one what's doing all this bad business. But never at yourself. Every man Jack on this estate and for miles around knows how good and hard-working you are. As for your garden, 'course you want to protect it. Each one of them little beds of plants is like the babe you ought to have to your breast. Now if Sir Harry had been any kind of a proper husband—"

"That's enough," Lea rasped, aghast at Suderanne's tirade, aghast at what she'd almost revealed before Dursten of the relationship she'd guessed accurately to have existed between Lea and Sir Harry. Lea's eyes darted to Dursten. He watched Suderanne in a serious and thoughtful way, not even a glimmer of the disapproval or amusement in his face Lea had expected to find there. His gaze wandered to the window and beyond, and his voice sounded as distant as the grey horizon he studied.

"It may not be necessary to have your garden razed. That quotation from Exodus prompted me to examine the brick in the walkway and rear wall in your garden, the only brick areas I could find there. Breaking random ones in half yielded nothing. I'd thought perhaps some precious metal might be hidden in bars in the centers. Then it occurred to me that something of value might have been mixed in with the materials used to make the bricks, especially those deeper yellow ones. Lord! What a job of retireval that would entail. Nevertheless, I had pieces chiselled out of any number of bricks and the resultant samples dispatched with one of my men to London. That fellow was ordered to ride hard, so he should return by tomorrow afternoon at the very latest with the assayer's report. I suggest we sit tight until then."

"Your logic is impeccable," Lea said softly, "and it all seems to fit. The bricks mentioned in Exodus, the implication in this quotation we've just found that whatever it is we seek may be used for an apparently mundane purpose. But I remember so well the making of those bricks. It was done here on the estate right at the start of our creation of the garden almost twelve years ago. That was long before Sir Harry had converted his assets into whatever form they take today and long before any idea of a Treasure Hunt Game could have entered his mind."

Dursten merely shrugged as if the futility of his idea and effort meant nothing. That gesture made Lea feel strangely apologetic when she could have felt superior, even allowing herself to gloat a bit over her rejection out of hand of any such obvious ideas as his. She found herself making excuses for him, reminding herself that she had a wealth of information he lacked entirely. Her voice was wistful as she spoke again. "I'm afraid there's no alternative but to put that army of men to work with shovels out there."

185

He waved his hand in dismissal of her words. "There's yet another turning before we have to take that avenue. Don't know why I haven't thought of this before because it's been obvious to me that dates are crucial, especially since I had to formulate the instructions about tracking Sir Harry's transactions which I sent two days ago from here to a firm of London inquiry agents." He paused and cocked a humorous brow at her in reminder of that time when she would have turned him into just such an agent.

"But Mr. Kerr has runners investigating."

"Kerr," Dursten said contemptuously and finally—there was to be no discussion on that subject! "What we must do, Lea, is put together a list of work done in your garden. And to be on the safe side of work done anywhere on the estate during the time shortly after we know Sir Harry began to liquidate his shares and holdings. We might have to talk to workers in the house and on the grounds because some building projects from the 1812 period might be unknown to you. And it is building projects I'm sure we're most interested in."

"Some project around here unknown to Lady Lea? That would be right funny," Suderanne scoffed, "since even five years ago she and that old steward was the ones that looked over near-about everything that was done here."

"Your testimonials to the industry of your mistress are effective, to say the least. Anyone within hearing would have to feel a sloth by comparison, myself included." Dursten grinned at Suderanne. He actually grinned. It was disarming and, to Lea, unbelievable. This stiff character unbending to jest with a maid? Incredible! And equally incredible was his apparent desire to help her find a way to spare her garden. At once Lea was put on guard. She measured her words carefully.

"Isham Burton has been pursuing a similar route or he was . . . before Thomson was attacked. I don't know if he was trying to connect dates with events exactly, but he's an alert man and I'm sure he's factored them in."

The remnants of good humor were wiped from Dursten's face. "Really?"

"Yes. Only hours after we'd found those fragments in the grate in Nigel's room Burton came to the house to see me and tell me that he was trying to help by inquiring among the workers and servants about any activity years back which might relate to Sir Harry's having the fortune shipped in or buried in the garden. Despite my anger with him a short while ago, which showed more the state of my nerves than anything else, Burton is an excellent man, a man I've trusted and counted on for these three years he's been here. Of course he would try to be of any assistance he could." She took a deep breath and plunged into a difficult confession. "You and Burton are of like minds in being direct about things. The failure of my attempts to find the clues and follow out their leads shows that you were probably right all along. You *did* suggest more 'businesslike' methods, I know."

A staccato rap at the door immediately followed by Blaecdene's entrance put an end to whatever response Dursten was about to make.

"Your pardon for bursting in this way," his words were clipped, and the curt nod he gave acknowledging the chaotic state of the bedchamber deterred him not a second. "Thomson is reaching the crisis point. He feels feverish and is tossing restlessly. I thought you would want to be at his side, Lady Lea. He's barely at the edge of awareness, but still he might know you were there."

"Yes, yes, certainly," Lea said quickly. But before chasing Blaecdene across the hall, she turned back. "We must go ahead with your plan, Lord Dursten.

Suderanne, please see Mr. Burton at once. Tell him what has happened with Thomson." She shot a quick look at Dursten. "I assume you want to be at the bedside as I do at this moment." He shook his head affirmatively, and she continued with her instructions to Suderanne. "Explain to Burton that his Lordship and I will be conferring with him as soon as we're able about the various projects that took place on the estate within the last five years." She started to leave, but halted again, almost bumping into Dursten who was right behind her. "Much as I would like to save my 'quaint all-yellow garden,' as you called it, I can't in good conscience now. So I feel we must put a time limit on your strategy. Shall we say until sunrise tomorrow? That gives less than twenty-four hours, I know, but if you have no first-rank leads by then, we shall start the digging. Suderanne, tell Mr. Burton that, also, and have him assemble a group of at least fifteen men, properly equipped to be at the ready for work tomorrow morning." She dashed away, disregarding Suderanne's roars of protest that the plan for digging should't go forward, that the men wouldn't even know what they were digging for!

Dursten strode ahead and opened the door for Lea. Thomson, who had lain so still so long, writhed now, emitting horrible, agonizing sounds that tore at Lea's sympathies. She flew to the bedside to assist Blaecdene in restraining Thomson and untangling the bedclothes his tortured body fought as if they were the assailant who had struck him down. As she worked with Blaecdene and Dursten, who had seen that his help, too, was needed, she was startled by Thomson's visage. There was a fragility, a delicacy to his face that was almost ethereal. Lea feared his end was near. She sucked in her breath on a sob and clung to the old retainer's hand as if she alone could pull him back from the brink.

Thomson's torso arched back against the pillows to remain rigid there while his breath came punishingly in a long sort of gasp. At Lea mute inquiry if this was the death rattle, Blaecdene slowly shook his head from side to side.

"How insignificant, how futile we are," she murmured before closing her eyes on a fervent prayer for Thomson.

"Did you hear that?" Dursten's sudden voice sounded overloud in the sepulchral quiet broken only by Thomson's pitiful wheezing.

Lea frowned.

"He seems to be forming a word," Dursten explained. "Syllables anyway. But I can't make it out."

Lea went taut with alertness. Indeed, Thomson did seem to be trying to communicate, for he made the same or very similar sounds over and over and over. Was it a word? Two words? It sounded like two. "Stach" . . . "Who" . . . "Sta-a-a" . . . "Choo."

All at once Dursten leaned close to Thomson. "Statue," he breathed into the man's ear. "You are trying to say statue, are you not?"

Thomson went on with his painful repetition as if refuting or not hearing Dursten who then looked over to Lea. "You try it," he prompted.

"Thomson, my friend," Lea said ever so gently. "You are saying statue. Is that right?"

He did not, indeed could not, respond, but within seconds the gasping of those syllables stopped and within minutes he was resting quietly again much as he had before this frightful interlude.

In half an hour Thomson's color had risen and his

breathing definitely was better, beginning to sound normal even. Blaecdene fairly whispered his verdict then that he believed the worst had passed, that he had some hope again for Thomson's recovery. Soft though the words had been they carried far enough for even the elderly Mrs. Runyon to hear and make known she had heard by jumping up and doing a quite uncharacteristic little jig of a dance. Dursten came over to Lea, drew her from her chair and retreated with her to a far corner of the room.

"My God," he said feelingly, "that poor man was so desperate that I can only hope 'statue' has some meaning for you in all this."

Lea was taken aback. Dursten sounded quite genuine in the emotion he expressed, and in a trice she was convinced to disregard the caution that tickled at her mind.

"There's only one way to tell—to get out to my garden and examine the statue that houses the fountain at the west wall. There's no other statuary in the garden, and nothing special in the house that I can think would answer."

"Well?" he asked, but he gave her no time to answer. He tugged her by the hand, none too gently, and sailed her out of the room and through the house. Only when they'd reached the picket fence did he release her, indicating she would precede him through the gate and along the brick path. But his hand was soon upon her again. She stumbled on a hole where a brick was missing, and only Dursten's quick, strong grasp saved her from taking a spill.

"My wretched workman must have forgotten to replace that after we did our tests," he grumbled, still clutching her bare upper arm.

His touch was maddening, sparking images and sensations of that one and only other time Dursten had been with her in the garden. She couldn't stand those unbidden memories, those unbidden sensations that tingled through her, and she wrenched out of his hold to run up the path. She stopped at the barrier of rosebushes banking the pool and placed her hands at her tiny waist as if contemplating the problem before her. In truth she was contemplating Dursten's curious effect on her, wondering if he guessed what his touch did to her and wondering, too, if she were some sort of love-starved creature whose sensual appetites were aroused by the first attractive man to stay under her roof since her husband's death. Humor was her only defense and, as she heard Dursten's steps come to a halt behind her, she strove for it.

"I'm afraid there's nothing for it but to defy those thorny monsters."

"I'll make the frontal assault through the thorns and over the pool while you advance through the thinner plantings at the back." The lightness of his tone matched hers and prompted her to wonder if it were equally false. She forced herself to play on.

"Very gallant," she called as she circled to the wall. "But do wait until I've turned off the water. No need to add the insult of a soaking to the injury of the thorns."

"By the by," he said as the splashing ceased and he stepped gingerly into the rosebed, "what do you think we're looking for?"

"I haven't the foggiest notion. Anything unusual about the statue, I suppose."

"Ah, then you believe it should have been an antiquary—not an assayer—my man sought out in London?"

"H-m-m, I doubt it. Of course I'm no expert, but to me the statue doesn't appear that great a work of art.

Fine, of course, but not from the chisel of an old master . . . or even a young one. No, what I'd been thinking was that there might be a hiding place within the statue and that we might look for a spring or hinge."

Dursten, to whom the statue was a new object for study, paused before going around the pool and looked over at it carefully. "Offhand, I'd agree that it's a good piece, but not a valuable relic, much less a masterpiece, so a cache spring I'll look for." With exquisite balance Lea would not have believed of a man so large, Dursten walked foot over foot like a tightrope walker along the edge of the pool to reach the statue.

"I'm afraid you'll have to examine the head and shoulders." Lea peeped around at Dursten, a rueful smile on her lips. "Too high for me." She began to run her hands over the muscled back and arms of the man in marble, sleek and wet from the water that glistened on its opalescent surface. Working her way down to the base, she crouched amidst the roses, feeling the squelch of wet earth as it began to seep through her thin kid slippers. Her fingertips glided over the cool smoothness of the sculpture and came to an abrupt, fluttering halt at the touch of raised lettering.

"An inscription," she cried, furiously scrabbling at the hurtful branches of the musk rosebushes, unmindful of the scratches they were inflicting. Dursten, his foothold precarious on the slippery edge of the pool, inched around to join her. They cleared away enough of the plantings so they could sit back on their haunches and decipher the lettering.

"Of course, of course," Lea whispered. "I think I knew even before we came here."

The base of the statue read: *Fidus Achates.*

Imminent wealth or the meaning of this statue to Sir Harry's legacy of puzzles, or any number of things might have filled her mind at that moment but, oddly, none of them did. She turned eyes misted with tears to Dursten.

"He *didn't* forget the present to commemorate my study of the *Aeneid*. That dear man, that generous man. He never reneged on a single promise he made me."

As the threatened tears spilled down her cheeks, she pushed herself up with the steadying aid of the statue and retreated. Dursten followed her out of the rosebed. Disregarding her emotion, he asked bracingly, "What does that statue signify?"

"Loyalty," she choked, "faithful friendship, promises kept."

He made a sound of disgust. "Come, come. You know perfectly well what I meant. What does it tell you of the location of the treasure?"

She was tired and frazzled, she knew, and her mind refused to work on anything save her emotions. Dursten, pressing her, made her snap. "Only that if nothing turns up in your work with Isham Burton, the musk rosebed should be the first area spaded in the morning." She turned to go.

"And suppose we find nothing," his voice came ominously low over her shoulder. "Sir Harry left you comfortably off with the manor and the income from the farmlands. You're not in want. Leave aside for the moment the subject of the would-be thief, and tell me how much further *you* will go with this search."

Lea stopped dead. For the first time in days, her mind darted to the future, not to bemoan the situation and think of leaving Gravetide as she'd done at Thomson's bedside. But to the real immediate future. To her and Winifred living alone at the manor after everyone had left. For whom would she work beyond the tenants and laborers? For whom would she matter beyond a few servants? Rushing into the lonely void came the image of children, lots of children. Her project of adopting a family out of Lambeth House of Asylum was even more important to her than it had ever been before. She wheeled to look up into Dursten's face, and with a voice made fierce from the need she felt for those children in her life, she told him, "I *want* that fortune and I will *have* it!"

Contempt made his lip curl, derision colored his voice. "Do you yearn for the high-life in London or the low-life in Paris, my good, hardworking Lea? Poor little Lea loaded with responsibility from the cradle? Did you put your dragon of a maid up to that passionate speech? Don't bother to answer, you false wench. You'll get nothing but your charming pastoral life as long as I hold your pursestrings. And in three years, my lovely, I have the certain feeling you'll be so broken by your experience under my hands, that you won't have the heart for an attempt on either of those gay citadels, Paris or London."

"You swine," Lea gasped before marching away from the volatile man she was sure now she loathed and who loathed her. A new and frightening thought about Dursten crept into her mind. In the suspicion and hostility he held for her was lack of reason and sanctimoniousness . . . two qualities that very well could motivate him to seek the treasure so that it might never reach her hands, hands he considered to be those of a soiled dove. Lack of reason and sanctimoniousness might even lead him to believe—since Sir Harry had appointed him trustee for reasons unknown—that he, not she, was the one "the fortune really belongs to."

16

"Suderanne here?" Isham Burton peered through the crack in the bedchamber door Lea had opened at his knock.

She shook her head in answer and frowned, mildly surprised that he would seek out Suderanne again so soon. They must have been talking long over the messages she had sent.

"Been out working for the last two, three hours," Burton explained defensively, downcast. "Come back a few minutes ago to find a big note from Suderanne tacked to my office door. She said she had to see me urgent-like. And that's what brings me here. Wouldn't have come up otherwise." He shifted uncomfortably. "Know where she is?"

Lea felt the first pricks of alarm. She hadn't paid the slightest attention to Suderanne's absence when she'd returned from the garden. She'd expected her to be away carrying the messages to Burton. Nor had she become unduly upset some half hour later when one of Dursten's footmen had come in search of pantry keys in Suderanne's possession and reported that a look around the house hadn't located the maid. Now with Burton's words, she was growing more and more apprehensive.

195

"I haven't the least notion where she is, Mr. Burton. One of Dursten's servants said they'd looked through the house and couldn't find her." Lea gulped. "Where could she be? Oh, where could she be?"

"Go on now. No need for such alarm. Suderanne's a right busy one always. She's probably flittin' around taking care of some dust back in a deep corner or doing some errand or such-like. You know her." His face crumpled into a frown. "Come to think, it might of been her I seen going up that path forking away from the front of the house. Anyways, I saw twixt the yew branches a mob cap like the one she wears, and that old cap was darting along in the direction of the ruins and the ice house. Want I should take a look?" He paused a fraction and then added quickly as though he, too, were worried suddenly, "If they're saying she's not to be found in the house, mayhap it's best if I organize a gang of men to do a proper search rather than wasting time and making a fool of myself running to ground some miss and her young man. With your leave, I'll get to that straight away."

"Yes, yes," Lea said hurriedly, her "thank you" barely audible as the door clicked shut behind Burton.

She paced. What could have happened to Suderanne? Why had she not come back directly after leaving the note for Isham Burton? She stopped on a sudden realization. Mob caps like the one Suderanne wore were really quite out of fashion. Burton, a man who scarcely paid attention to such things, couldn't be expected to realize that. It was ludicrous to think any young girl visiting Gravetide would allow herself to be seen in such a monstrously out-of-date headdress, and there was no other woman who worked in or near the house who wore a cap like Suderanne's. It *had* to have been Suderanne he had seen moving along the path.

But what conceivable reason could she have for going to the old ruins or to the ice house?

The ice house! Lea clapped her hands to her cheeks. So aware of the crucial importance of dates of building projects from the discussion with Dursten and the messages carried to Burton, Suderanne must have remembered the ice house and gone to investigate. Of course she would think of the ice house! Asked to recall a building project at Gravetide within the last five years, a hundred people on the estate would answer immediately, "the ice house." Its design and construction had caused quite a stir, drawing people from great distances to see it. Built of strong brick—yet another reason Suderanne might consider it—and burrowed deep into the ground, the ice house would endure for centuries, or so Sir Harry had proclaimed upon its completion. Nothing short of a catastrophe, the major upheaval of an earthquake could destroy it.

Despite the fact it was not in the Yellow Garden, the ice house would seem a great possibility as the hiding place because of its fastness and because of the dates of its construction. The excavations for its deep vault had taken the whole of the summer of 1813. Its construction had stretched through the fall, but it finally had stood ready for filling in the early winter of 1814. Lea could reason as Suderanne must have. The time of building might be a bit late, but not unreasonable. Sir Harry might have collected the proceeds of his liquidation, begun in 1812, in a bank vault in London and had the money shipped out upon completion of the ice house for hiding there. A very good theory . . . if one weren't convinced the treasure was in the Yellow Garden, if one didn't know about Thomson's most recent direction to the statue there.

Lea swiped at the gauzy curtains at the windows

letting onto the front of the house and looked down on the driveway. Her eyes traced the path threading through the yews and beyond where it was lost under a canopy of trees. There was no sign of Suderanne. No glimpse of that mob cap, common in an earlier day and time, saucy now and distinctive as Suderanne's badge.

Dark grey clouds clotted in the dingy sky. The sun, invisible as a distinct sphere, shone no one place and all places at the same time, its light seeping through the thick, dull heavens to bathe the landscape in ubiquitous liquid pewter. Not only was Suderanne on a wild goose chase, but about to get a complete drenching, judging by those threatening clouds. From the clothespress Lea snatched an oilskin pelerine, voluminous enough to shield them both, and left the room on a trot.

During her quick progress through the house she was aware of flashes of azure and scarlet. She was becoming accustomed to the many footmen Dursten seemed to find necessary to the orderly running of a household in which he stayed. It was only when she reached the entrance to the path through the yews that she became suspicious. Turning on a hasty idea that Suderanne might have bypassed her and even at that moment be entering the house through front, side or rear entrance, views of all of which the placement of the path permitted, Lea saw a footman startle at her turn, then appear to idle by the door through which she'd just passed. She thought there was something familiar about the man, that she had seen him before, outside her bed-chamber door on one occasion, near Nigel's room. . . . But it was impossible to tell. All the footmen looked alike which, of course, was the very purpose of livery and powdered hair. The powdered, starkly styled hair especially served to extinguish individuality, to help in creating a cadre of nearly identical-looking ciphers who could be forgotten, who could be ignored ... anonymous drudges never presenting themselves as individuals who might deserve consideration or concern for their opinion on what they might overhear. But, even as Lea *couldn't* be sure this was the same man, she *was* sure and her hackles rose. Dursten's spy. Well, she would lead that bird dog a merry chase. And she did, whipping off the path and taking a parallel route a few yards west that was a series of broad, moss-covered stone steps up the gentle slope. She entered the gardeners' tool shed at the top of the knoll and immediately exited through a door on the other side, doubled back to the east and slipped through a stand of trees and down to a break in the yew hedge. Keeping under the shadowy limbs of the yews to avoid being seen from above, she darted along the path to the ice house, placed for convenience not too far distant from Gravetide Manor.

Built into a hillside, the ice house showed to the passerby only its outermost set of arched double doors within a grassy frame. The doors stood ajar now, a quick assurance to Lea that Suderanne was within because normally all three sets of double doors in the vaulted passageway leading to the large well where the ice was stored were shut tight.

Lea grasped the pull and used her weight to lever back one of the solid oak doors, a foot thick and heavy as she was. Opening it enough to get through comfortably, she shouted in.

"Suderanne, are you here?"

Her voice whistled down the vault and bounced back from the cold, sweating bricks. She called again, taking halting steps into the murky passage as her eyes struggled to become accustomed to the darkness. The second set of doors was closed. She hurried to them, strained to move one on its enormous hinges, then poked her head into the gloom beyond.

"Where are you, Suderanne?"

The odor of damp straw and with it the faintest smell of fish assaulted her nostrils. Cold perked up from the chasm filled with the blocks of ice sawed the winter past from the lake near the manor and from ponds dotted over the estate. The frigid air nipping at her cheeks, her hands, her feet seemed to be pouring through the last set of doors. She shivered and drew the pelerine more tightly around her while she squinted ahead. Extraordinary! The barest filterings of grey rays outlined the hinges of the doors near the domed ceiling and a great maw of blackness where the doors should have stood fast. Those doors really *were* up.

Though covered in gooseflesh and desperate to retreat from the chill, she forced herself forward to investigate and if necessary and if possible to close the doors. They were sloping doors, ingeniously arranged with a pulley wheel and rope to which was attached a large wooden crate for hauling up and lowering ice in the vault. There were strict orders that all the doors, particularly this last pair, were never to be left open when not in use. Annoyance with a worker who'd neglected this essential task was wiped out of Lea's mind with the swooping thought that Suderanne might have met with an accident.

Lea rushed forward, calling Sunderanne's name urgently as she went. And, too late, premonition—or more likely her senses—made her try to stop and reverse her movement on the frost-slippery incline to the great gaping midnight hole . . . indistinguishable suddenly as the whole tunnel became midnight with the thud of the second set of doors closing at Lea's back.

She groped for safe footing, for a hand-hold as well. A thrill of sheer terror shot through her. She could hear the person who had laid this trap gliding away from the doors he'd just shut and toward her, a huge night-gifted animal, his body responding, almost anticipating, each feint to right or left of her own body. Blind in the inky cold, blind in the panic driving her, she lurched wildly from one brick wall to the other, back and forth across the passage from which there was no escape save the desperate plunge down into the ice cavern. A soft, gloating laugh shimmered in the boreal blackness, a confident sound coupling with slow, deliberate shuffling steps to tell her there was no retreat for her and no salvation.

As if gripped by the paralysis of nightmare, Lea stood rooted against the wall, arms flung out stiff in desperation to keep away the menacing figure inching toward her surely and steadily. Shivering, she was swept with trembling waves of sickness while her heart pounded hurtfully against her ribs and her head swam giddily from fear. Warm, sour breath fanned her face. She gagged in revulsion and fright. Hard hands, savage hands swept under her outstretched arms to grab her brutally, thumbs gouging into her breasts until she shrieked with pain and was wrenched away from the wall. She struggled frantically, clawing at the brute arms that entwined her. Her feet, slipping and sliding on the slick floor, were suddenly churning futile air as her nemesis lifted her and began to move inexorably toward that yawning mouth of the ice well.

Even as she divined her fate, it was upon her. With a grunt of effort its designer, its instrument hurled her into the shaft. She pitched head over heels through void, flailing at nothingness, brain benumbed and registering curiously the cries tearing from her throat as if from another, detached and distant. She struck the wooden crate dangling in mid-air, its rope pegged above but not counterweighted so that it came plummeting with her. In one last gesture at survival, she batted the wood away so that it would not crash on top of her as she hit the ice.

An explosion of pain ripped her head to toe— searing daggers along her spine, white-hot needles in her head, a stiletto of fire in her middle taking the breath out of her body with its thin scalding blade. She lay insensible, unable to move, barely able to suck air into her tortured lungs, and winking from oblivion in to dazed awareness and back into oblivion again.

It was the cold creeping along her limbs, pricking her face, stinging her nostrils and throat that brought her round. Moaning, she forced herself up on hands and knees. Her ears roared. Her head was cotton batting. Her stomach somersaulted with nausea. She was covered with straw, the straw that rested on top of the ice, the last, the uppermost of the straw that was between each of the dozens of layers of blocks of ice beneath her. The straw scratched her delicate skin, poked hurtfully through her thin dress and into her abused body. But she gave that straw no damns, only mute thanks, for it was the accident of landing on an exceptionally thick bed of it that, she realized dimly, had saved her life.

The cold, an ally only monments before, had metamorphosed into her enemy and caused her to draw on her last reserves of strength and intelligence. She was freezing. Her teeth chattered. Her body quaked with the piercing cold. She dragged herself over the ice, scattering straw as her raw palms searched for the pelerine separated from her in the downward flight. When at last she found it, she collapsed in a fit of weeping. The storm of tears helped, lessening her shock, relieving her pain so that she could go on. She scavenged straw, scraping it together, drawing it from every corner until she had piled before her almost every scrap that had lain over the entire floor of ice blocks in the vault. She embraced the straw, clambered up on it, then flattened the top to make a resting place. It was almost three feet thick. She stuffed her pelerine with it and snuggled deep within, hugging her legs to her bosom and rocking gently side to side. She was cold still, but not freezing any longer, and she stopped her motion as a delicious lethargy began to steal through her. Soon a strange sense of peace pervaded her thoughts, her emotions.

Lea felt safe, cherished, rare as the ice in summer. Buried together, she and the ice, cut off from outer air by the three heavy sets of doors in the entrance passage above, they were protected deep in the blackness underground, insulated first by the thickness of the brick walls of the vault and then by the tons of earth all around. Dreamily, a smile touching her bluing lips, she wondered if it would be a month or more—one of those steamy days in late July, perhaps—when someone at Gravetide might feel in need of an iced cream or a frosty drink and, sending a servant to fetch one of the frozen blocks, she would be discovered. The notion didn't disturb her. Nothing did. She couldn't even care a fig about the identity of the person who'd lured her to the ice house and thrown her into this pit. She couldn't think on trouble, only on misty memories of past happiness—romps with Sir Harry, rides with the old steward, duets played with her father on the little pianoforte in their cottage.

She burrowed deeper into the straw. Ah, she *was* so like the ice. The wind could not touch her, nor the heat of the sun. The elements could not render her from this exquisite diamond hardness into the common stuff of running water. Running water. She imagined herself in miniature, a doll floating in the pool in her Yellow Garden. Her face was washed by the cool green water splashing softly over the shoulders of *"Fidus Achates"* peering eternally down at her, his expression benign. Abruptly Sir Harry and Thomson broke upon the web of fancy her mind was spinning. They fished her out of the pond, gently wiped her dry, bundled her in quilts and propped her up on the tawny marble bench to watch them drain and clean the pool. Thomson and Sir Harry always had done that chore together without help from the servants. It was a biannual ritual. The clues swam together like a school of tiny minnows, then darted apart. She chuckled, the sound reverberating eerily in her frigid tomb. Really, she thought with lazy amusement, it was all so simple—the nature of the treasure, its "hiding" place. She should have discovered it eons ago. It was a pity she never would be able to do so now. She experienced mild regret, but not real suffering at that thought. How could she suffer? She was so wondrously comfortable . . . so delightfully drowsy . . . so utterly at peace.

17

It was outrageous, infuriating even, the incessant calling of her name, the repeated abrasive slaps to her cheeks, the continual chafing of her hands. How dare anyone harrass her in this rude way! She refused to be awakened and turned her head from side to side to evade those stinging hands until one of them clamped down on her mouth. Her lips were pried apart. Raw, burning spirits washed her tongue, poured into her swollen throat. She choked and came bolt upright to a sitting position, spluttering, gasping. Catching her breath at last, she subsided with a groan back into a nest of rough blankets, smelling vaguely of horses.

Lea was all throbbing flesh and nerve and bone. But it was her head that was the worst of all—splitting with pain, contained thunder and lightning threatening to shatter the vibrating bones of her skull at any second. She couldn't focus her eyes, and the figure swimming in murkiness above her was recognizable only by his country-accented voice saying her name and by the work-callused hands with which he tried to soothe and revive her.

"Ah, Isham, I should have known you would be the one to find me." Her voice was a croaky whisper. "You know the estate like the back of your hand and all of us on it equally well. I was wrong, you know. Suderanne didn't go to the ice house. It was a ruse . . . a lure. . . ."

"There, there. You shouldn't be trying to talk." It sounded as though he choked back a sob. "I'm the one to hold to account for that. More fool me."

"Is it . . . is it night? I can't see too well."

"A fair night with a good moon."

"So the rain did come to clear the skies."

"More than rained, stormed—and hard—like it did a few days back."

She whimpered. "Then the roads will be muddy again. Washed out in places. Impassable. And *they* will stay. They will have to stay on here." Her words trailed off in a tone of despair.

"Don't fret yourself. I won't let Dursten agitate you no more. I'll take you away somewheres until he clears off the place and we can come back. Then we'll go on as before, only maybe better."

She tried to nod, but the shooting pains that came with movement were unbearable. If she stayed perfectly still, her head was all right—fuzzy, woozy, but all right.

"Howsomever, Lady Lea, we can't fly while Sir Harry's fortune stays behind for the likes of Dursten or worse, Mr. Nigel, to find. We'll have to take it and leave a note saying so. That way we'll save your pretty garden in the bargain, for Dursten's got a score of men at the ready to tear it up at sunrise. We can't let him ruin your very own place, now can we?" He crooned the question to Lea.

"Oh, no. We must save it. Yes, we must." Her brain was reeling, and she felt very helpless and small and incredibly grateful to Burton for his strength and his clear direction.

"Look here." She heard him rattle a piece of parchment. "I think I've found something will help turn up that fortune. An old paper fell out of a dusty ledger in my office this very evening. It's in Sir Harry's hand, and I think it's one of them clues."

Lea could make out a shimmering rectangle directly above her face. She groaned. Her eyes closed on the quavering image that brought dull throbs to the backs of their sockets.

"I'll read it to you," Burton said. "It says first, 'Pindar, Olympian Odes. I.'" Stumbling over the written words, forms so alien to him, he ground out two halting sentences:

> " 'Water is best. But gold shines
> like fire blazing in the night,
> supreme of lordly wealth.' "

"Where did Sir Harry bury the gold, Lady Lea. The gold what's called here the 'lordly wealth.'"

Lea wanted to laugh, but the sound that came was a grating noise far from mirthful. "Those lines confirm it, of course," she murmured. "But I knew before. I knew in the ice house, lying on all those frozen blocks." She shivered. "Where are we, Isham, outside? The air feels fresh, it smells sweet."

"On the little cleared space in the yew path just down aways from the ice house. But it matters not where we are. You must pay attention to the words and tell me where the treasure is buried. We've to make haste if we're going to get away before Dursten and all his flunkies find us."

"The treasure isn't buried. Never buried. Oh, but you are very strong, Isham, and you can carry me, can you not?"

He grunted. "You know I can."

"Then you must. You must carry me to my garden, to the pool there. And I will find the treasure in just the manner Sir Harry wanted me to." It seemed terribly important to her tortured mind, her confused feelings that she play out the discovery exactly as she imagined Sir Harry had anticipated she would. And when Burton balked, his voice coming harsh to her ears, she burst into tears, wails almost, and unaccountably loud for one in her feeble condition.

"Hush," Burton said swiftly. "Hush now. You mustn't give the alarm to those devils scouring the place."

She didn't understand his words, but she understood his strong arms sliding beneath her, lifting her to grant her request.

Burton walked very softly, but nonetheless with each careful footfall she knew shattering pain along her back. Her spine was made of glass, and jagged shards were splintered away from it with each jolt to stab into the base of her brain. She gritted her teeth, her breath coming ragged, but she forced the screams of anguish to die in her throat, for she had to get to her garden. It seemed an eternity of suffering before they reached the gate, a nightmare of torment as Burton jounced her when unlatching it.

She transcended her pain on a wave of rapture as they moved slowly through the garden, transformed for her by her blurry vision and the shimmering moonlight into an ethereal bower. "For where your treasure is, there will be your heart also," she whispered. The flowers, stirred by a soft breeze, seemed insubstantial as gossamer and equally delicate and lovely. Burton set her down on the rim of the pool, as she requested. The water, basin, facings trembled before her poorly focusing eyes like a beautiful illusion, the statue a phantom hovering above. *Fidus Achates.* She addressed the statue in the tones reserved for the loved. "A faithful friend is a strong defence and he that hath found such an one hath found a treasure." She smiled tremulously at the marble man, thanking him for guarding so well Sir Harry's fortune. Tentatively, so as not to provoke her pain or destroy her dream, she slid her fingers into the pool to make gentle circles in the water. She cupped her hand and raised it, letting the water trickle slowly back into its home. "Water is best. But gold shines like fire blazing in the night, supreme of lordly wealth."

Her hand trilled across the water, creating ripple upon ripple in the little pool until she withdrew it so the water could subside into glass-like stillness. "Look beneath the surface," she said so low that Burton was forced to bend double in an effort to hear. "Let not the several quality of a thing, nor its worth escape thee." She peered unseeing into the water and as if through it to the basin of the pool. "And straw I did not give, but the lordly wealth."

"Are you all right?" Burton asked sharply.

"H-m-m, you sound as though you think I'm mad. No, I'm quite sane, I believe." Her vague, dreamy eyes sought Burton's face, but could not fasten on it and drifted away. "Dear Sir Harry, always so suspicious of his relations, of banks, of investments. Always safe-minded was our Sir Harry, wasn't he, Isham? I mean, it was quite true to his nature that he chose this form for his fortune. I should have guessed from the first, of course."

"What form? What are you talking about?" Burton asked impatiently.

"Why, Isham," Lea said as if talking to a deliberately stubborn child, "gold. You knew the lordly wealth was gold. You told me so only moments ago." Her forefinger flipped a path through the water. "Sir Harry *would* want gold. Indestructible. Calamity-proof. The metal prized above all others."

"You mean it's stored beneath this pool?"

"Not beneath. It *is* the pool. Don't you see? Look at the little bricks that form the bottom, sides, facings of the pool. They're not just gilt-*colored*, they are gilt. Sir Harry had his gold cast into shallow ingots that look like bricks . . . or perhaps he bought them in that form . . . no, I rather think he had them cast. They fit so perfectly."

"My God," Burton rumbled. "How are we to make off with all this?"

Lea laughed, and this time the sound came out right. "Sir Harry would never arrange things so that a sneak thief could make off with his fortune in the night." And she laughed again, a soft little melody of laughter.

"Are you crazed from that fall? There's nothing bloody funny about this predicament."

"I am a bit strange in the head, aren't I?"

He snorted and stretched up to his full height, looking angrily down to the pool. The moonlight slanted across his compact body.

"Why, Isham Burton, what are you doing fully dressed at this time? You should be wearing night clothes like all the others."

His face went taut. His eyes burned into her. "What are you saying?"

She was befuddled, time and dates and places intertwined in her thoughts. She spoke very slowly, like one dimwitted. "Well, it was past two o'clock in the morning. Everyone else had on nightgowns and robes. You were the only one there in the hall, crowded around Thomson who hadn't changed, who was dressed in the same clothes you had worn at dinner."

"My game's up with you, eh?"

Sudden, intense disappointment jerked Lea a fraction closer to reality. "Why did you do it? Poor old Thomson. He never deserved such an ugly attack."

"That snivelling prig!" Burton exploded. "I think he saw me fixing to sneak into your garden when Dursten was in here mauling you . . . and you looking like you was enjoying it," his voice was harsh with angry scorn. "First I'd thought only to spy, to see if you'd guessed what the treasure was and where and would go to it. Then it came to mind to scare you, get you off on another direction, not that Dursten hadn't already took you body and soul off somewheres else. I had to trip you up by burning the clues, too. Mr. Nigel thought he was so smart gathering them together like a pack rat, but anyone half-smart can see right through him and everything he's doing. It was him gave away the treasure was here in this garden in the first place. I had to put hindrances in the way of all you people disadvantaging me with your book learning. I couldn't figure the clues and such-like. I only had my hands and my raw wits to work with." Burton's fingers threaded through the shock of unruly brown hair spilling onto his forehead. "Thomson's a tough old bird. He'd got plenty suspicious when I went begging information from him. I knew he'd put two and two together about me and was going to spill it out. I couldn't have that, Lady Lea. No indeed."

She'd sobered a bit, but everything still seemed quite unreal to her. She was utterly unafraid. "Put hindrances in my way, scare me in my garden, scare me with a warning note." She sing-songed the words before turning to a cross, severely chiding tone. "How you could ever think to frighten me into running! Surely you know me better than that?"

"Stupid. You're right. Just got your back up. But I didn't want—" His voice broke.

As if scolding a truant, Lea continued. "And lying to me about this last clue. It didn't fall out of any dusty ledger; you found it in the search of Sir Harry's room. But most of all, Isham Burton, it was too, too bad of you to try to steal. How dare you think of taking something that doesn't belong to you?"

An animal sound of frustration and hurt erupted from this throat. "You think it don't belong to me? Me? Sir Harry's own flesh and blood. His son. If it don't belong to me, it don't belong to nobody!"

His words penetrated her daze and made her gasp. But his revelation was overtaken by sounds of shouts and commotion in the distance. Lea's eyes swept to the east, to the entrance to her garden and beyond. "I can't make that out," she said plaintively. "There seem to be dozens of stars twinkling on the horizon, but they're much too low."

"Torches," Burton said tersely. "Torches being carried by all them what's looking for you. My guess is they'll be upon us in another few minutes. Not that they haven't searched this garden half a dozen times already. They keep coming back to it over and over again."

With an enormous effort, Lea dragged her thoughts back to the words Burton had spoken before this intrusion.

"I really don't understand how you can say you're Sir Harry's son. He was never married before. He never acknowledged you as his son."

"You think with a beautiful, innocent young thing like you around he was going to so sounding off about his bastard?" He laughed harshly. "Not likely. But a bastard I am and an Asher I am. That much I had from the Burton family what raised me. Why else do you think Sir Harry would come hot-footin' it all the way to Sussex and our little farm and drag me back to Gravetide so's he could have me train for steward. Damned little training there was 'cause in a few short weeks he'd pensioned off the old steward and you and me was going it alone running the place, if you remember."

"I couldn't forget, Mr. Burton. You'll never know how much I fretted over Sir Harry's treatment of the old steward. Don't misunderstand, I admired your abilities and still do, but Sir Harry was so abrupt, almost cruel to that old gentleman who'd given his best to Gravetide for so very long."

"And did you never wonder why Sir Harry picked me up and carted me back here."

"Fleetingly. But then Sir Harry's actions seemed transparently obvious when you turned out to be so good at the work. Your predecessor was getting very old, too." She was distracted by the noise of the searchers and looked in their direction before turning back to Burton an innocent, guileless face. "What are you planning to do? They're getting very near, you know."

"Run off, taking you with me. They'll not harm a hair on my head with you in my grip."

She absorbed this placidly. Deep within there was a rustle of fear, but it was too remote to prompt action or words calculated to save herself. She spoke truthfully what was in her clouded mind. "I don't know if it will work, Mr. Burton. Somehow I don't think I can survive more than a few minutes of being jostled about." She shrugged ever so slightly and winced at the shooting pains that gesture caused. "And a corpse won't offer you much protection, I fear."

All the vigor went out of him, and he dropped to his knees to take her hands in a rough clasp. "I never meant to hurt you so bad, Lady Lea. Never meant to hurt you at all. I was just going to get you out of the ways for a while so I could hunt for the gold. And so's everyone would be looking for you and not thinking on anything else. I near went out of my mind when Suderanne comes to me and tells me Thomson was thrashing about and you and his lordship had decided to work together and if all failed to start digging up the garden. Time was running out for me. But I swear I was only going to shut you up in the entrance part of the ice house, never shove you down the hole."

"I know, I know," she comforted him. And she *did* know he hadn't meant to hurt her, she also knew the reason he had. "I shouldn't have ordered you out of the house, should I? It spoiled everything. You couldn't keep an eye on Thomson or me, couldn't listen for something that might help."

"All of that and more. I went crazy wild with rage that you talked down to me in such a way for you'd never used a hard tone with me before. There you was slappin' me back low when I was thinking to rise up. Then I got blind mad again in the ice house."

"Oh, Mr. Burton, how easy it was to hate a faceless, nameless menace. How I could revile the monster who'd attacked Thomson, how I could despise the craven person who'd written that note. The anger felt . . . well, almost good. But *you*, knowing it is *you*! It feels terrible, terrible." Tears of pity and compassion washed her cheeks. "I am so sorry."

The winking torches were no longer bobbing on the horizon, they were flooding into the garden, beginning to illuminate Lea and Burton in tableau at the edge of the pool. His head was in her lap, and he was weeping as she was. But at the muffled shouts of discovery from the lead footmen, he shot to his feet. His eyes were wild and, heedless again of Lea's well-being, his arms flung out, snatching her up and holding her as a shield before him. She screamed with agony. Then Dursten's voice cut the loud babble engulfing her, and there was a tumult of fierce words flowing between him and Burton, fierce words Lea couldn't follow, so great was her pain. She believed there was a remarkable change in that torrent of words and that Dursten was begging for her release, pleading that Blaecdene be allowed to tend her, but it couldn't be—the great Lord Dursten using that humble tone to a steward and on her behalf . . . never!

She tried to shout, but her voice was a scant whisper. "You must let Isham go . . . go in safety. In truth the gold belongs to him. What he did he did only because he is Sir Harry's son."

"In a pig's eye," a scornful voice rose from the crowd that swayed dizzily before Lea.

"Is that you, Nigel?" she asked wanly.

"It is. And Burton's no more Sir Harry's son than I am, though he is an Asher. A bastard Asher."

Lea heard Winifred scream, a long, piercing wail of shock turning into an anguished stream of "no" upon "no." It came to Lea just whose son Burton was and the pathetic nature of that secret about which Nigel goaded Winifred, the girlhood shame she had wanted desperately to keep from everyone. And it came to Burton, too. His gutteral cry was as wrenching as Winifred's.

"Never her bastard, never hers." His hands tightened on Lea's shoulders. "Say you forgive me," he demanded. "Say you understand, Lady Lea. I wanted everything Sir Harry had because I thought he was my father and it was rightful mine."

She strove to gather the strength to utter the words

of absolution he craved, but even as they were forming on her lips she was lurching forward, falling into waiting arms as Dursten and several of his men rushed Burton. It was Blaecdene who'd been assigned her care, who held her safe and tight and knelt with her right where he'd seized her. She was foggily aware of a struggle behind her, of Burton being subdued, then dragged away. But overall there was Blaecdene moving her down to the walkway, placing her flat on the ground with only a cloak beneath her. His examination was swift, sure with firm though not ungentle hands. He concentrated on her eyes, lifting the lids and playing a torch from side to side, staring into her eyes as he did so. He called for a stretcher.

"We've seen this condition all too often after a heavy artillery barrage," Lea heard Blaecdene reporting in muffled tones to a giant who loomed above her. "Brain shock. She'll have to be moved with the utmost care. It's a miracle the blood didn't burst in her brain with that ruffian handling her in the way he did."

There was a thundering oath from that giant to whom Blaecdene spoke. "How could I have entrusted her protection to a footman? I should have done the job myself, and this would never have happened. Are you sure she'll survive?"

"Quite sure and without permanent damage, I believe. But she'll need total rest, probably for no less than a month, and absolutely no more upsets of any kind."

The stretcher was brought up. Lea cried out as she was lifted and begged for the blessed oblivion of unconsciousness, but she was not to be so gifted. She felt every inch of her pain-wracked body and could not restrain the moans that tore from her throat.

With another violent curse Dursten halted the stretcher bearers and gathered up Lea in his arms. With

216

infinite care, infinite patience, he inched through the garden, the house, up to her room. She felt not the slightest pain as he lowered her onto her bed, keeping his arms under her for long minutes before withdrawing them ever so slowly and gently. His face was very close and she saw a perplexing expression there, an expression of mingled sorrow or disappointment and tenderness or regret.

"Blaecdene says you are not to be in the least way disturbed," he said in a very low voice. "I want Blaecdene to see to your nursing. You do trust him, don't you?"

"Yes," she murmured.

"Very well. He shall stay behind while I'm off to London in the morning." His mouth twisted in a wry smile. "Your recovery will be all the more rapid, your convalescence happier with me absent from under your roof."

There were no controls on her thoughts or her tongue. "Much happier. You are very disturbing to me, you see. You misunderstand so cruelly." Her mind drifted off and it was as if she were speaking to herself. "H-m-m, more it is the sensuality I find difficult to cope with, to understand fully. If I'd ever known a man—"

Dursten's fingertips slipped softly over her lips, silencing her. "I will leave you and," he faltered and his last words sounded angry, "with an apology."

She reached out a detaining hand. "But you will not go until you see to the dismantling of the pool and the storage of the gold, please? Suderanne said—" She felt a quickening of worry. "Suderanne! Burton didn't——"

"I'm here, deary." The maid crowded closer to the side of the bed opposite Dursten. "Burton trussed me up and stuck me in his rooms over the carriage house, but he did me no real harm. And I made such a fearsome

217

racket after I wiggled loose a bit, that I was rescued in no time. I'm right as rain and you've no cause for the least alarm."

"I'm so glad, so glad. Poor Isham. He . . . he was demented there at the end." A tear trickled down her cheek. "You were right, Suderanne, right as always. He wouldn't have done any of it, if it hadn't been for the temptation. We must have the gold in a proper, safe place, lest someone else have his devil escape."

"I'll see to that," Dursten said curtly.

She started to explain about the hiding place, but Dursten cut her off. "We've all the detail we need from Burton who was muttering about the pool as we hustled him off. The pool and the clues, it is obvious now."

"Don't let any harm come to Isham," Lea said. It took an enormous effort for her to continue to speak. "The courts are unjust, vicious. He didn't actually kill anyone, and there are mitigating circumstances."

"I think everyone must leave now," Blaecdene said firmly. "Lady Lea must rest. She cannot go on this way."

Dursten bent low. The words he whispered in Lea's ear would stay with her for months to come, though when she was fully recovered she would wonder if they had not been part of her ravings.

"I've been a blundering, inept fool and every kind of a rotter," he said. "And as Burton begged your forgiveness, so do I."

18

The halcyon summery day was a surprise coming as it did after a fortnight of weather that had been chill and damp, a mist forming each evening to cloak the next dawn in a pearly haze. The fog burned off early this mid-October morning and the temperature soared, auguring not just one, but a spell of St. Luke's summer days.

Dignified and unruffled as ever he had been, Thomson ushered an unexpected visitor up the winding path of uneven stone steps and across a patch of browning grass to the picket fence. Swinging open the gate, he stepped back apace to permit the Earl of Dursten to enter the Yellow Garden. After a formal bow, which hid the twinkling in his eyes, Thomson withdrew.

The air was fragrant with the pungent smell of autumn flowers. In half a dozen beds along the brick walkway, Michaelmas daisies nodded creamy heads, their bright yellow faces smiling in all directions. A stand of Showy Coneflowers, golden and tall, preened in the brilliant sunshine proclaiming merit of their name while behind them, rising almost five feet and going back deep to the side fences, were primrose-colored Autumn Suns. But it was the chrysanthemums from the large-flowering variety down to the button-blossomed ones that dominated the garden with their spectrum of incredible yellows, lemon to deepest saffron.

The garden might be alive with flowers, the creatures they drew, and with sparkling sunlight, but it seemed devoid of the human occupant Dursten had been told he would find there. With swift annoyance, he turned to call Thomson to an accounting, but a pull at his cuff, followed by an insistent tug at his sleeve brought him round to peer down at a tiny girl. No more than three years of age, the tot appraised him with profoundly blue and solemn eyes. At length his questioning frown was answered by a flickering of a smile at the corners of the bow mouth in the little face upturned to him. Apparently the child approved of what she saw, for her smile broadened and dimples appeared in cheeks glowing with health and vitality.

"I'm glad you've come to play with us," she gave her verdict plain, while slipping her hand into his.

He was about to tell her that, indeed, he had not come to play, but his words were lost in a shriek that issued from somewhere to the rear of the garden.

"Harriet, Harriet," came a shrill, gleeful voice, "I've found our Lea!"

For the first time in his adult life, Lord Dursten found himself captive of a child. His would-be playmate had him firmly in tow and pulled him in the direction of giggling voices.

"I should have won," she gently reproached him as they neared her objective, "had you not interrupted my seek."

Having no proper apology at the ready for such a situation, Lord Dursten wisely remained silent and allowed himself to be tugged toward the rear corner of the garden. Sitting on a square of soft turf surrounded by tall flowers were a small boy and Lea. Little tendrils of curls clung damply to Lea's forehead, and an unmistakable smudge on the cheek set off her flushed face. She rose in confusion. She hadn't set eyes on her trustee these five months past, since he'd left her bedside that grim night in May.

"Lord Dursten! What a complete surprise to see you!"

"And you, Lady Lea, are ever the surprise to me." There was a hard edge to his voice as he added, "Am I to conclude that congratulations are in order? Suddenly and without my knowledge you have taken a widower as a husband?" He looked pointedly at the children.

"Our Lea isn't married," the little girl piped, still holding tight to his hand. "At least she isn't anymore, because dear Sir Harry is in his grave, you see."

"I'm afraid I don't see, young lady."

Recovering from her shock, Lea said quickly, "Allow me to introduce my wards, Lord Dursten. The little minx holding your hand is Harriet and my friend here is Julian." The children performed their curtsey and bow most gratifyingly, but as Julian straightened he looked puzzled.

"We're not what you called us—'wards'—we're your 'dear little children,' that's what you told us."

"And so you are," Lea laughed, hugging the small brown-haired boy whose soft curls set off a pair of stunning grey eyes. "But you are also my wards, which makes you twice as important."

Thus soothed, Julian clapped his pudgy hands and announced merrily to Dursten, "Our pretty Lea is going to give us another brother and sister."

"Within a sennight," Harriet added importantly.

Dursten crooked a brow at Lea. "What a remarkable female you are," he observed drily.

Lea felt a blush steal furiously over her face. "Children, run find your Aunt Winnie and tell her we shall have a guest at dinner. Then ask Suderanne if you may visit with baby in the nursery." The children scampered away as Lord Dursten asked in astonishment, "Baby? There are more about?"

"Oh, yes, our baby is the dearest fellow. We just got him. He's only three or four weeks old and we're entirely thrilled with him. The older children came in early July, as soon as I was truly well enough to receive them. I've renamed them because it was so dreadful what they were called before. The little boy was 'John Eleven' because there were ten Johns in the orphanage before him; the little girl was 'Mary Nine.' Now he is Julian, called after my father and she is Harriet, after Sir Harry, of course. The baby—" She broke off and turned ever more rosy wondering how Dursten would react to a namesake. Little Collin up in the nursery had arrived with no name at all.

"What on earth is all this?"

"It is my project. The project for which I needed Sir Harry's fortune." She drew a deep breath. "My heart's desire for ever so long has been to see Gravetide a big jolly home. My children are foundlings from the Lambeth House of Asylum."

He received this explanation with an expression of deep thoughtfulness. "I should have guessed it was something along these lines."

"No you shouldn't. It is a wildly unorthodox thing to do, I'm told, so how could you be expected to guess?" She was disturbed by Dursten's surprise visit, but even more disturbed by the troubled look in his eyes, the faint haggardness she thought she detected in his face.

"Lea," he said her name without formal address in the most sombre of tones, "it takes an extraordinary amount of time to rid oneself of a preconceived notion, no matter how ill it sits."

She chose to interrupt as well as misinterpret his words. "Ah, you think of the treasure and everyone assuming it was buried. Quite true. If I hadn't let my mind be filled up with that idea, but left free to range over the possibilities, I'm sure I would have found it straight off. It was so obvious! Sir Harry was like a school boy filled with relish, with zest for the pool building. The recollection of his verve in executing the project, if not its date, should have led me to the correct conclusion at once. Preconceived notions are hardly a defense, though. It is more rank stupidity and blindness on my part——"

"Taking a page out of Suderanne's book, I won't let you get by with castigating yourself in the least. There was Burton playing his brute game, Nigel behaving like a fool with his Aunt terrified he was the villain and hovering about anxious to cover up the least suspicious thing that might be attributed to him. But I am to blame most of all, for I was your greatest obstacle, upsetting you, falsely accusing you. I was very wrong and I can admit it now."

Lea knew the confession was extremely difficult for him. Irrelevantly, she wondered if he'd ever before apologized to anyone. His intensity set off the most wild sensations in her, and she sought desperately for a change of subject.

"How rude of me not to have thanked you on first sight for all you've done. Your letters have been most encouraging, and the new steward you sent to us is working out splendidly. There was, too, the safeguarding of the gold and intervening with the court on behalf of poor Isham Burton. I'm so glad he got only transportation to New South Wales. Without you I fear he would have been hanged. My testimony, the testimony of a woman, wouldn't have carried much weight. And then there is your title, your position which are so influential."

"Perhaps I should have let the scoundrel hang," he said bitterly. "I only intervened because you wrote requesting me to do so. But, blast, the man nearly killed you."

"I shall never believe he intended to."

"And you don't think he returned to the ice house to rescue you out of sheer desperate need for your help since he couldn't turn up the fortune even with that clue he'd found?"

"Perhaps. I think he wanted everything Sir Harry had, all right, but there at the end——"

"At the end he wanted you more than anything else. You may be right." He smiled wryly. "There were so many bloody quotations in this whole affair that I hesitate to mention the one that came to me at the last."

"But you must!"

"From the Bard." His voice was very low. "Beauty provoketh thieves sooner than gold."

He fell silent. After a long interval in which Lea's nervousness had grown to the jitters, she forced herself to smile and say lightly, "I suppose you've come to see the steward and check our accounts which, I can assure you, are in perfect order."

He shook his head. "I wrote you I would never check your accounts nor try to limit your freedom in any way." His eyes bore into her. "I came only to see you."

She swallowed hard. "Well, see me you do! And perfectly recovered. Dizziness and headaches persisted for some time, and it was difficult for me to remain still as I was told I must, but I did. And the result is quite happy."

"Blaecdene reported you were a fidgety patient, too anxious to be back to your old, vigorous routine, but he said you were a good patient, nonetheless."

"Dear Blaecdene. I've written him, of course, but you must give him our best regards. We miss him dreadfully, for we all grew quite fond of him the six weeks he remained with us to nurse Thomson and me."

"He mentioned a spot of effort with Lady Winifred, too. I suspect he was unduly modest on that score."

"A *spot* of effort? My word yes, that is modest. I can't conceive what would have happened to Winifred without him. He was a paragon of patient understanding and kindness, winning her confidence and trust. She was so distraught, determined to leave Gravetide and what she thought to be her final humiliation here. It was only Blaecdene's calm guidance that led her to see things differently. Imagine if she'd actually gone back to the Carey-Browne household! It was there, you know, that her father sent her when she was 'disgraced' by the young man with whom she thought her self in love. He ran off. Oh, horrid story."

"I know. Nigel gave me an earful. One point in particular was cleared for me—Lady Winifred's obsessive attachment to that unpleasant young man. Made perfect sense when I learned Nigel had been born under the same roof and one scant month after her own child."

"It appears she transferred to him all her frustrated maternal instincts." Lea studied the toes of her slippers for a moment, then looked up at Dursten. "She never saw her baby, you know. She was heavily dosed with laudanum and the infant wasn't shown to her . . . just whisked away."

"So of course she couldn't know of the birthmark. But Nigel told me he had that from his father. Unbelievable Nigel could be such a dunce that until the night

225

in the garden he didn't put together the fact Lady Winifred's baby had a mark with Burton's appearance and fathom the reason Sir Harry had brought him here to be steward. Incredibly dim, Nigel."

"But incredibly bright at times, too. Remember the deduction about Thomson's and Sir Harry's use of *'Fidus Achates.'* " Lea chuckled. "I'm afraid the true nature of Nigel's 'grey matter,' as he unceasingly refers to his brain, will be always an enigma."

"I will be grateful if the whole of that young man remains forever an enigma to me—an enigma at a very great distance from my person." His words sounded hard, but there was good humor in his expression. "You've set him up handsomely in London."

"I tried to provide sufficiently for all the Carey-Brownes and for Lady Winifred." Lea was wringing her hands. She had tried to be conversational, but she couldn't keep it up. The tension within her had risen to an unbearable level. She gathered her courage. "Lord Dursten, why have you come here? Certainly not for this chit-chat about matters of five months and more in the past."

He straightened and looked away briefly. Lea's heart lurched. Dursten's expression was apprehensive. For one mad moment she thought that the wish she had on that first day of meeting to see him grovel before her might come true. And she knew with a sickening certainty that it was the last thing she would ever want now. She put a gentle hand in his.

He exhaled sharply. "Lea, I'm a damnably arrogant, domineering man. A flawed man who finds it almost impossible to express tender emotions, but tender emotions I have, though they were damned near schooled out of me by my father and the harsh tutors in his employ. He was terrified I might have inherited the

226

slightest amount of my mother's promiscuity of feeling and was determined to eradicate even the imagined trace——"

"I've heard a bit about the scandal," she interrupted in a soft voice, anxious to relieve his pain. "Don't distress yourself further."

"Distress myself *further*?" he exploded. "God Almighty, I wonder if that would be possible? I have been more distressed in the last five months than I ever imagined possible. Lea, after all the unforgivable, wretched rudeness, the insults I heaped on you——"

It was her turn to explode. "Oh, do be quiet on that score. You apologized even before you left, if I remember rightly. I'm quite able to understand the catalyst for your suspicions. I *am* young to be the widow of such an old man, and even now we haven't the least idea why Sir Harry appointed you co-trustee. But, really, I find it rather excessive in you to wallow in self-reproaches."

He took a step closer. "Don't you understand, Lea? I want to tell you I love you. The first moment I saw you I fell in love with you from here"—his finger tickled the tip of her retrousse nose before tracing a tingling path up to the bridge—"to here." He chuckled hoarsely. "Yes, I fell in love with you . . . with each feature, each trait I discovered in you. Fool that I am, I wouldn't admit it even to myself."

Her heart was pounding ferociously. In the time they'd been apart, not an hour of a day had passed without Lea thinking of Dursten, and his attractiveness for her had grown alarmingly. All she could manage was a strangled echo of her normal voice. "We . . . we will have terrible times and glorious times trying to get on with one another, but I don't see how we can do otherwise than try."

With a shuddering groan he drew her into his arms.

After ushering Dursten into the garden, Thomson had made his way with deliberate speed to the house, through it, and up to the corner bedroom at the back. Its mullioned windows, cranked wide to admit the glorious warmth and freshness of the unusual autumn day, permitted full view of the Yellow Garden. He had never been one to spy or snoop, but on this special occasion he allowed himself the rare break from his customary integrity of conduct.

Thomson watched Lea and Dursten as they gestured in conversation and remembered sadly Sir Harry's premonition, confided to him alone, that he would not live past his bride's twenty-fifth birthday. Leaning on the sill to observe Lea taking Dursten's hand, Thomson recalled with a rueful shake of head his doubts they'd ever come together after taking such an instant and violent dislike to one another. He looked even more closely as the two figures melded into one in a passionate embrace. He was flooded by his memory of the obverse emotion to the one he witnessed. Hate and the growing sense of danger from one unprincipled player of Sir Harry's game. How he'd failed to put an end to it, but almost had the end put to him. As the passionate embrace of the two in the garden showed no sign of ending, he turned from the window.

Fortunately no one trod the passage outside the bedchamber to hear Thomson's chortles of glee, such exceptional sounds they would have startled out of wits any of those persons beneath Gravetide's roof who thought they knew him well. Nor did anyone hear the words Thomson directed at the ceiling and beyond.

"Ah, Sir Harry, it turned out—with a few unforeseen and unfortunate twists along the way—just as you'd hoped, just as you'd planned for your Lea and Dursten. You always was a managing old devil, Sir, if you'll forgive my saying so."